CHRISTMAS PERIL

Elizabeth Penney

Annie's®
AnniesFiction.com

Books in the Sweet Intrigue series

Library of Congress-in-Publication Data
Christmas Peril / by Elizabeth Penney
p. cm.
I. Title
            2020948711

AnniesFiction.com
(800) 282-6643
Annie's Sweet Intrigue™
Series Creator: Shari Lohner
Editors: Jane Haertel and Lorie Jones

10 11 12 13 14 | Printed in China | 9 8 7 6 5 4 3 2 1

Christmas in Castlebridge. It sounded like a television movie title. Kara Foxworth slowed to take the exit ramp off the highway and released the breath she hadn't been aware of holding. Traffic had been horrible tonight, with a steady stream of other holiday travelers leaving the city and heading into Vermont for the holidays.

At the foot of the ramp, Kara stopped to let a few cars pass. A crescent moon was rising, flirting with her through bare tree branches etched against the sky. She turned onto the winding rural route leading to Castlebridge. She still had thirty miles to go, driving past sprawling farms and through towns barely big enough to support a general store and post office. But she was almost home.

Her phone rang. Kara checked the screen and saw it was her mother. Using the hands-free system, Kara answered. "Perfect timing. I just got off the highway."

Her mom laughed. "I figured as much from your text when you left. How are the roads?"

"Busy on the highway but clear and dry." She was grateful that the promised snowstorm had held off. Driving on slippery, snow-covered roads was never fun, but it was even worse at night.

"I'm so excited that you're staying for almost two weeks," her mother said. "I've got all kinds of plans."

Kara was an elementary school librarian in Massachusetts, and this year, Christmas break was longer than usual.

"Like what?" Kara laughed. "Household projects?"

An ongoing source of teasing between them involved the tasks her mom asked her to do when Kara came to visit. Not that Kara minded. A widow for more than a decade, Michelle Foxworth had been struggling to maintain the family home. She had a tight budget, which meant that she hired a handyman only when absolutely necessary.

"No—oh, who am I kidding? I have a couple. But they're small." Her mother paused. "But I was talking about the Castlebridge Christmas Days celebration. It's going to be so much fun. I dug out the old family cookbook and bookmarked some recipes."

"Peppermint candy canes and thumbprint cookies?" Making cookies and other goodies together was a childhood tradition, and Kara loved it. They also used antique cutters to make classic sugar cookies and embellished the various shapes with frosting and sprinkles.

"You bet," her mother said. "I already bought all the ingredients."

It was wonderful to hear her mother sounding so happy. After the loss of her husband, Miles, twelve years ago and the disappearance of her sister-in-law, Angela, two years later, her mom had struggled with depression. They were huge losses that blew holes into a happy little family. The memories were especially painful around the holidays.

Miss you, Dad. Miss you, Auntie Ange.

"I'll be home within the hour," she said. "Although I might stop and grab something to eat." Eager to get on the road, she hadn't bothered to eat before leaving her apartment, and now her stomach was growling.

"Don't do that," her mom said. "I'll heat up some shepherd's pie for you."

The dish containing ground beef, creamed corn, and mashed potatoes was another childhood favorite. "You're spoiling me."

"That's what I'm—"

The signal vanished, a common occurrence due to Vermont's hilly terrain.

Kara laughed. She could call her mother back in a few minutes or wait until she got home to talk. Cell phone service was spotty between here and Castlebridge, and it often cut out in isolated spots where it was really needed.

More than once she'd wondered about her aunt, who had disappeared ten years ago. Angela had driven away one day in her car, and she'd never been heard from again. No calls. No letters. Nothing. Kara was afraid that something had happened to her in one of these dead zones, where help couldn't be summoned.

She forced away the thoughts with a shiver, knowing that once she opened the box, they were difficult to contain. The worst part of it all was not knowing the truth. If Angela was dead, it would be tragic and heartbreaking, but at least they could mourn. Instead, they lived with the torture of wondering where she was, if she was okay. If she had run away with a man, like the rumor mill said.

In the deepest recesses of Kara's heart, she knew that Angela would never, ever have left without saying goodbye.

Kara drove on, recognizing familiar landmarks as she drew closer to home. The line of huge old maples arching over the road. The unique round barn standing in a field. The covered bridge spanning the Castle River, which wound its way through Vermont to meet up with the much larger Connecticut River, which ran through four New England states. Kara remembered dropping sticks from the smaller stone bridge in town, imagining the twigs floating to Long Island Sound on the Connecticut shore, then out to the Atlantic. In reality, they probably hadn't made it beyond the town line, but it had been fun to think about.

Her phone rang, and her mother's name flashed on the screen again. She pushed the button to answer. "I lost you, but you're back."

"I am." Her voice was garbled, wavering in and out. "... hear me?"

"Not very well," Kara said. She realized she had raised her voice as if that would help.

"They . . . Angela—"

What? Kara had just been thinking about her aunt. She tensed in her seat and forced herself to concentrate on the road, her heart pounding. "Aunt Angela? Did she come home? Did she call you?"

". . . found her—" The line disconnected.

Kara tried again and again to redial. *Emergency calls only* flashed on the screen. She had no service at all, not even one bar. She hit the gas and sped up as fast as she dared go, hoping she would soon reach a spot with a strong signal. And then she would pull over and call her mother.

With both hands on the wheel, she drove over rolling hills and around tight corners, grateful she knew these roads well. She glanced at the dark woods pressing close on both sides as she kept watch for deer or moose or even a dog. Creatures had a way of darting out into the road without warning, and such collisions could be fatal. For humans as well as the animal.

She checked the service bars illuminated on the screen. Nothing. Where was there a signal around here? She tried to picture the surrounding landscape in her mind, remembering that there were towers on some of the higher peaks. But it seemed that for the last several miles she'd been in a very big dead zone. She noticed her battery was getting low, so she plugged in her phone to charge.

One last long hill marked the approach to Castlebridge. Kara's small sedan climbed, shifting gears automatically. Still no signal. At the top, she tapped her brakes, preparing for an equally winding descent. This road had claimed many a life over the years at night, in bad weather and good. The woods were even thicker here, the tops of tall trees blocking any light from the sky. A deep ravine channeling the Castle

River ran alongside the road, and after storms and in the spring, the water roared and tumbled over big boulders far below.

It was quiet and partially snow covered now. But the curves and corners were still dangerous, and although the urgency to get to her mother made her desperate to floor the gas pedal, Kara slowed as she approached the most treacherous spot in the county.

Dead Man's Curve.

Where, many years ago on a December night much like this, her father had crashed his car and died. The road had been dry and clear, the moon almost full. Nothing had malfunctioned on his vehicle. The brakes and the steering had worked. But to this day, the police had no good answers concerning the accident.

First her father's death. Then the mysterious disappearance of her aunt. How much tragedy could one family take? Once again, Kara wondered if the two were connected. But then she hastily dismissed the thought. If they were, surely the police would have figured that out.

Blue lights flashed in the treetops. A chill ran down Kara's spine. Those weren't cheerful holiday lights. Had there been another accident? She drew in a sharp breath.

Around the last corner she slowed to a crawl. Several cruisers, an ambulance, and a fire truck were parked on both sides of the road, and a large tow truck was smack-dab in the middle of the left-hand lane. The groan of a winch could be heard even through her closed windows.

She rolled down the window, oblivious to the frosty air rushing in. Someone had crashed on this dangerous corner. Exactly like her father. Kara bit back a sob. Another family torn apart. She prayed whoever it was would be all right.

Orange cones had been set up to block cars from driving through the site, and she pulled to a stop.

A man appeared in her headlights, crisscrossed neon tape on a vest defining his body. He stepped closer, gesturing with a lighted baton for her to drive on the shoulder to skirt the scene.

But something held Kara in place. She watched in fascination as the winch continued to *whir*, as it struggled to haul a vehicle out of the woods. With the window open, she could hear the shouts of officers as they directed the operation. Metal crunched and wood cracked as the object hit slender trees along the slope. Police floodlights hit chrome, then glinted off a crumpled green hood.

Kara opened the car door, the sight of the wrecked vehicle stealing her breath. Her mother's words flashed through her mind. *Found her.*

The man directing traffic strode toward her car. "You need to move on," he barked.

"No," Kara protested, walking forward on wobbly legs. "I need to see." The world narrowed to the tow truck and the vehicle crashing out of the woods. *Angela, no, please, no—let me be wrong.*

The man blocked her. "Get back in the car. You need to drive on."

Barely hearing him, she pushed past his bulk, focused on the automobile attached to the tow truck.

With a final grind of the winch, the vehicle came fully into view. A green Toyota sedan. Exactly like the one Aunt Angela had driven.

A woman's scream pierced the night, easily carrying over the *whir* of the winch.

Officer Sean Colton whipped his head around, searching for the source.

His heart clenched. Kara Foxworth was struggling with a firefighter, doing her best to push past his bulky figure. He couldn't believe she was at Dead Man's Curve tonight of all nights. They were right in the middle of an operation to retrieve her aunt's car.

And her body.

Sean had been one of the two officers assigned to check out the wrecked vehicle, reported that afternoon by a hiker who had lost his dog. They needed a confirmed identification and an autopsy from the medical examiner, but the rusted license plate matched, and the skeleton's remaining garments and belongings were consistent with the last known description of Angela Foxworth.

Angela had been reported missing ten years ago. At that time, Kara had hated Sean for breaking her heart. She probably still did. They hadn't really spoken since high school.

"Can you take care of that?" Chief Mark Colton asked, tipping his head toward the altercation. His face was set in grim lines. "We don't need a lookie-loo on-site right now."

"Yes sir," Sean told his uncle, not bothering to add that he'd been about to approach Kara. Or that Kara wasn't a lookie-loo—she was a family member. Perhaps of all of them, she had the most right to be here to witness the confirmation of the sad fate of her beloved aunt.

Instead, he trotted toward Kara and the fireman.

"Let me by!" Kara shouted. "That's my aunt's car."

The firefighter gripped her by the shoulders. "I can't allow you to go over there. It's a crime scene."

"No kidding it's a crime scene. But none of you believed us." Kara kicked the firefighter square in the shin.

He dropped his hands with a howl.

She darted past him and ran directly into Sean.

"Easy." Sean grabbed her by the shoulders. It was the same move as the firefighter, but at least he had a valid excuse. If he hadn't caught her, she would have fallen and smacked her head on the asphalt. Once she was steady on her feet, he let go. Not that he wanted to, he noted ruefully. He had a sudden urge to wrap her in a hug to comfort her, but he'd lost that right a long time ago.

Kara, still swaying slightly, peered up at him. "Sean?" Her gaze skittered over his heavy police jacket and uniform, her upper lip curling. "Of course you're here."

Sean would never tell her that he'd been first on the scene. She didn't need that thought embedded in her memory. And he didn't blame her for her resentment toward the local police department. Although he and Kara had been estranged, he had heard enough gossip to know that people in town hadn't taken Angela's disappearance seriously. They'd believed she'd run off with a man.

And what had he believed? Uneasiness twisted in Sean's gut. He hadn't jumped on the bandwagon that painted Angela as irresponsible and impulsive. But he hadn't defended her either.

Sean had to put his own doubts and musings aside. Kara needed his help. "I understand where you're coming from," he said gently. He gingerly put an arm around her shoulders and ushered her away to a quieter spot.

"Do you really?" Kara leaned against him, a sweet weight that felt so right in his arms. She began to sob, deep, rending cries that shook her slight frame.

Oh boy. Sean dug around in his pocket for a handkerchief, grateful he'd grabbed a fresh one that afternoon. He handed it to her and pulled back to give her room. The separation felt like peeling away skin.

He winced, wondering what was wrong with him. This was a grieving family member, not a potential date. Not that Kara would ever date him again.

"I can't believe it's her," Kara said. "In the same spot my dad died."

Cold shock washed over Sean. How could he have forgotten? Miles Foxworth had crashed his car here one night and suffered a fatal injury. His car had gone off the road, and he'd hit a huge tree.

Was there a connection? Sean's trained mind automatically considered the possibility. Law enforcement professionals didn't like coincidences. They usually pointed to the truth.

But at the moment, his mission was to send Kara on her way so the responders could do their work unimpeded by civilians. Behind them, the grind of the winch stopped, but the briefly deafening silence soon filled with shouts. A vehicle approached from town, and Sean recognized the medical examiner's SUV.

The chief would have his badge if he didn't send Kara on her way—and fast.

"Listen." Sean slung an arm around her shoulders again. "I know you want to find out what happened to your aunt. I do too. But right now, we need to do our jobs and go over the scene very carefully."

In the flashing lights, her wide, dark eyes pierced him. "I'm not an idiot. I know all that. After all this time, the last thing I want to do is mess anything up. You all spent a decade doing that." She folded her arms across her chest. "I don't want to hear any lies or evasions or any theories that this was my aunt's fault. Because I don't believe it. Promise me that you'll tell us the truth, no matter what it is. We've been waiting ten years for it."

Even though objections immediately popped into Sean's mind concerning the conclusions that might be drawn or his ability to share sensitive information, he found himself nodding. "I'll do what I can. Please go home. You and your mom will need each other. I'll call you later."

Kara stepped away. "I'll hold you to it. You better believe it." Before he could ask how to get in touch, she added, "Our home phone number is in the online directories." She stalked back to her car, not once glancing at the wrecked sedan, which now had a tarp thrown over the windshield.

"Was that Kara Foxworth?" the chief asked Sean after she drove away. "Talk about bad timing."

The medical examiner was now with the body, preparing to move Angela to the morgue.

Sean inhaled, anticipating resistance to the question he wanted to ask. "Do you think it was an accident, Chief?" While on duty he always called his uncle by his title, even if his uncle didn't always return the courtesy. The one or two times he'd slipped, the chief had scolded him, telling him that he expected respect and decorum.

"Absolutely. She went off the road at high speed, and her momentum carried her down into the ravine." The chief furrowed his brow. "Don't start spinning any conspiracy theories on me. The simplest answer is usually the correct one."

Sean decided not to press the issue. A team would be reconstructing the accident, although after a decade, much relevant evidence had been lost. Scars on trees and tracks through the undergrowth had been obscured. The same could be said for skid marks and tire tracks on the road surface. They'd have to dig out historic weather records to find out if the pavement had been wet or icy.

"Why do you think no one discovered the car until now?" he asked the chief. "Ten years is a long time."

Chief Colton rubbed his chin. "I've been thinking about that. Soon after Angela went missing, we had a huge windstorm. A lot of trees came down in this area. Must have blocked the view from the river." He shrugged. "They've finally decayed enough that you can get into the ravine from the river."

Which was low this year, thanks to a drought. A combination of weather events and time had led to the discovery.

The medical examiner had emerged from Angela's car and was making his way toward them. Peter Osbert was short and slight, and he appeared nerdy in oversize glasses. But the man was brilliant. "Chief," he said, pushing his glasses up with his thumb, "we'll need closer examination and positive ID, but the body is definitely female."

Sean had been expecting that, but his stomach still lurched. He'd gotten to know Angela very well when he and Kara were dating. Fragments of memories flashed through his mind—a pretty dark-haired woman smiling, laughing, and dancing in her kitchen. What a terrible loss.

"A fracture in the front of the skull appears to match the cracks in the windshield," Peter continued. "Preliminarily, you understand. But that may be the cause of death. Hard to say after all this time."

Chief Colton patted the medical examiner's shoulder. "I'm sure you'll be able to figure it out. Get this case closed before Christmas, so the family can put poor Angela to rest." His fleshy features conveyed deep sympathy and concern.

Sean winced, thinking of Kara and her mother. Putting a loved one to rest was never easy, and during a season that was supposed to be joyous and full of family, it would be even more difficult. He resolved to do what he could to help them through this ordeal. Kara might not want his sympathy, but he'd try anyway. It was the least he could do.

"Shall we give the order to transport?" the chief asked. "Once the ah, corpse, is cleared, I want my officers to do a quick search. Then we'll have the car impounded for a closer examination."

"You think she might have been impaired?" Peter asked as he and Chief Colton began walking toward the wrecked vehicle.

Sean followed on their heels, close enough to hear what they said.

"It's always a possibility," Chief Colton replied. "Sad to say."

Sean almost protested, but he thought better of it. The chief was simply following protocol. But Sean was pretty sure Angela never drank.

"That might explain why she went off the road," Peter said. "It's a dangerous curve under the best of conditions. Under the influence, a crash is almost a foregone conclusion."

Sean didn't like the direction this discussion was going. Between gritted teeth, he said, "Maybe an animal darted out in front of her."

Some of the anger he was feeling must have seeped into his tone, because Chief Colton eyed him thoughtfully. "I remember now. You dated the Foxworth girl. Knew her aunt, I'm sure. Maybe I should pull you off the team."

Peter put both hands up. "You two hash it out. I'll supervise the removal." He trotted off, calling to the EMTs standing by.

A hollow opened up in Sean's chest. He had to stay on the case. How else could he make sure that Kara and her mother got the closure they deserved?

"Kara and I are ancient history," he said, pushing aside the sweet memory of his arm around her shoulders. "My skills are needed on this. You know I've been taking classes."

Sean was working toward his criminology degree with the aim of becoming a state police detective on the force that handled Vermont's most serious crimes. That position would mean relocation, but he was ready to move. He had only his aunt and uncle here in town—his parents now lived in Florida, and he had no siblings—and opportunities on the local force were limited. Besides, after blowing things with Kara, he'd never found a woman around here to equal her. No, there was nothing keeping him in Castlebridge.

The chief regarded him for a long moment before finally nodding. "Put on some gloves and help Officer Cramer search the vehicle."

The ambulance was now pulling away, lights flashing but no siren.

Sean joined Ryan Cramer. The officer was young and eager, and he had a bad habit of always trying to one-up Sean. It was annoying. Sean hadn't decided if Ryan was merely competitive or jealous of the chief's possible nepotism toward Sean.

"Your girlfriend was pretty upset, huh?" Ryan asked as they pulled on latex gloves. "What was she doing here, anyway?"

"She's not my girlfriend," Sean said in what he hoped was a discouraging tone. "And she was on her way home for the holidays." He kicked himself as soon as he said it.

Predictably, Ryan made a jeering sound. "Does she know you're tracking her movements?"

"Officers," Chief Colton barked, "get to work."

Under the chief's watchful eye, the two officers searched the sedan thoroughly. As Sean fully expected, there were no empty liquor containers or other signs that Angela had been impaired. The dead woman's handbag held the usual—a wallet containing cash and credit cards, hairbrush, lipstick, loose receipts now decayed and illegible, and a couple of what might have been wrapped lozenges. Several library books were also found in the car.

Would someone as conscientious as Angela Foxworth leave town without returning library books? Sean didn't think so.

"We got nothing," Ryan said to the chief, showing him evidence bags holding the handbag and books.

"Check the trunk," Chief Colton said.

The trunk contained a spare tire and a set of tools, plus an adjustable snow shovel and a set of jumper cables, prudent items to carry during a Vermont winter.

The chief peered over Sean's shoulder. "This is it?"

"Yeah, typical trunk stuff," Sean said. "Want me to take any of it into evidence?"

The chief turned away with a grunt. "Don't bother. We'll be going over the vehicle more closely at the garage."

As Sean closed the trunk lid, he thought not of what was in the trunk but what *wasn't*. Rumor had it that Angela had left town for good. If that were true, then where were her suitcases?

Kara drove the rest of the way to Castlebridge on autopilot. Instead of raging with grief and anger, she was stunned. Frozen like the landscape that had hidden her aunt's car for so many years. She observed herself as if from a distance, both hands on the wheel, foot working automatically as she braked and hit the gas.

She had experienced this strange disconnect when her father had died. It had been weeks before the protective shell cracked and she began to mourn. Even now, the tears still came when she relived bittersweet memories.

Angela had gone off the road in the very same spot Dad had crashed. What did that mean? Everything—or nothing? How often did a dangerous corner claim lives from the same family during separate accidents? Hardly ever, she guessed.

And Sean . . .

She'd seen him around town when she'd returned to visit her mother, but they'd never really talked after high school, just waved perfunctorily from a distance. Now, here he was, in the thick of this horrible situation. His presence had been oddly comforting, almost as if he still cared.

Kara shook her head, trying to dislodge that thought. He was a good officer, and he would treat anyone the same way.

Houses were closer together now, announcing that she was almost home. Castlebridge was a typical small Vermont town, nestled between hills in a river valley. A century ago, brick mills had spun wool provided by nearby sheep farms. Today those old mills housed other businesses, sheep had been replaced by cows, and the town was highly dependent on Castlebridge College to bring visitors and commerce. Kara's mother worked in the college library, one of many residents employed by the institution.

As Kara drove down Main Street, she could see the college, a cluster of majestic granite and brick buildings set around a large green and illuminated by spotlights. Since Christmas vacation had begun, only a few people were crossing the green, their heads bent against the cold wind. The place had a deserted, eerie feeling.

In contrast, Main Street was festive, with white lights wrapped around trees and decorations hanging from lampposts. The mix of brick and clapboard storefronts were also festooned with lights, and store windows were decorated with seasonal displays. Every year of her childhood, Kara and her parents had strolled Main Street, shopping and drinking hot chocolate, during Castlebridge Christmas Days.

Which started tomorrow, according to a hanging banner.

At the end of the shopping district, Kara steered onto Elm Street. This route led to a grid of residential streets abutting the college. Some streets held grand mansions. Other streets featured more modest but still attractive bungalows and ranch-style homes. Kara's mother lived in an adorable Cape Cod exactly like the one next door, which had belonged to Angela. Since her aunt's disappearance, her home had occasionally been rented to visiting professors staying a few weeks or a semester. Judging by the dark windows and lack of a vehicle in the drive, it was currently empty.

Kara pulled into the driveway and parked next to her mother's blue Forester. *Home sweet home.* An evergreen decorated with colorful lights brought cheer to the small front yard. Garland had been twisted around porch posts, and a large wreath hung on the red front door.

Smoke lazily drifted from the chimney, which meant the woodstove was going.

Normally Kara would have jumped right out of her car and rushed into the house, eager for a reunion with her mother. But tonight something held her in place. Once she talked to her mom, all of it would be true. Angela was gone, stolen from them in a tragic accident. How would her mother cope with this devastating loss?

It was this last thought that forced Kara to move. She needed to be there for her mother right now, to be a strong shoulder to lean upon. Her mother didn't deserve anything less.

She grabbed her handbag and opened the car door, debating whether or not to collect her suitcase from the trunk. She might as well. Once she was inside the warm house, she would be reluctant to brave the cold to come back for it.

While Kara was pulling the suitcase out of the trunk, the front door opened.

"You're home," her mother said. She didn't even have a coat or hat on, and she wore slippers.

"Go inside. You'll freeze to death." Kara winced at her poor choice of words.

In response, her mom stepped farther out onto the porch, her arms crossed, waiting.

Kara quickly lowered the suitcase and pulled up the handle so she could drag it along, then shut the trunk lid. The knot in her stomach grew even larger as the moment of truth loomed.

"Did you hear the news?" her mother whispered as Kara lugged the suitcase up the steps. She followed her so closely into the house that she almost stepped on Kara's heels.

Once inside, Kara parked her bag and took her mother gently by the forearm. She tugged her inside and closed the door. "I did." She gathered her mother into an embrace. "I'm so sad." Tears burned in her eyes.

Her mom squeezed her back. "Me too." After they broke apart, she said, "Did you hear it on the radio? I tried to call you, but it kept dropping." Her eyes were wide, haunted with grief.

Kara nodded the lie. The memory of what she'd witnessed crowded into her mind—Angela's car being winched up the bank, the shattered windshield, the tarp hastily thrown over the front. But although her lips trembled with unsaid words, she knew she would never give them voice. Once she did, the horrible pictures would live forever in her mother's mind. It was bad enough that they would haunt her own dreams for years to come.

"I'm just about ready to dish up the shepherd's pie," her mom said, talking fast. Feeding people delicious meals was one of her coping mechanisms. "Come sit down by the stove." She practically pushed her daughter toward an overstuffed sofa placed in front of the fireplace with its inset stove. Behind glass, a fire crackled and roared.

"I'm not really hungry." *Anymore. Not after what I saw tonight.*

Despite her protest, the room's warmth and comfort drew Kara in, and she found herself collapsing onto the wide cushions. As she stared into the flickering flames, she dimly heard the rattle of dishes and her mom muttering in the kitchen. She always talked to herself, something Kara teased her about.

Her mother bustled in, carrying a tray. She set it on the coffee table in front of Kara, then moved a stack of magazines aside. The tray held a cup of coffee, a wide pottery bowl heaped with shepherd's pie, and two homemade rolls on a small plate.

"This looks great. Thank you." Kara picked up the mug of coffee, already doctored the way she liked it, with a splash of cream. The hot liquid was reviving, the fresh-ground aroma making her suddenly hungry again. She drank a long swallow, then set the mug aside in favor of the meal, one of her winter favorites.

Her mom perched on a nearby armchair and watched as she ate. She didn't speak, probably aware that discussion of the tragedy would ruin Kara's appetite.

Finally Kara set her spoon down. "That was so good. Best meal I've had since Thanksgiving." She'd had that celebration here at home, so she knew her mom would get the joke.

Her mother's brown-eyed gaze was unwavering. She was now in her midfifties. Her dark hair was threaded with gray, and gentle lines bracketed her eyes and mouth. But she was still slender and quick. It was rare to see her so still, as if she might break if she moved.

"I still can't believe it," Kara said. Maybe the fire had thawed her emotions as well as her body because the tears began to flow.

Her mother hopped off the chair and sat down beside Kara. She put her arm around her and drew her close. "Me neither." Her voice was husky. "For years I've wanted to find out what had happened to Angela. To think she was there all along."

Kara thought of her father's accident, and she once again held back the words. Without proof that the two tragedies were related, why say anything? It would only upset her mother more.

Her mom leaned her head against Kara's. "We can finally put her to rest. I'm so glad about that." On this last, her voice broke, and now it was Kara's turn to comfort her.

The two women sat like that for a while as the mantel clock ticked and the fire died down.

Finally her mom pushed herself to her feet. "I'm so glad you're home." She wandered over to the woodstove and poked the coals, then added a couple of logs.

"Me too," Kara said, grateful that she'd been here to share her mother's grief. She rose and picked up the tray. "Would you like a cup of hot chocolate?" That had been one of their rituals when Kara was younger.

"Sure." Her eyes lit up. "With extra marshmallows." That was another of their traditions.

By the time Kara returned to the living room, her mother seemed better. Yes, her eyes were still red-rimmed, but she was smiling.

"I can't believe you're here for two whole weeks," her mom said, accepting the mug. She blew on the cocoa to cool it down. "Castlebridge Christmas Days are going to be really fun this year."

Kara knew that celebrations were the last thing on her mother's mind, but she played along, knowing she was trying to make things seem normal. They talked about the parade and the downtown craft fair and the Christmas concerts.

Finally, when the clock struck ten, her mom declared herself ready for bed. "Don't bother with the dishes. I'll run the dishwasher tomorrow." She paused in the doorway to the hall. "You know where everything is. See you in the morning."

"I'll lock up," Kara promised. Despite being bone-tired, she wasn't quite ready for bed. She would sit in front of the fire for a while and think about nothing.

The crackle of a log settling roused her from a doze. The clock read almost midnight. It was way past time to go to bed. As she was getting ready to lug her suitcase up the stairs, she realized that her phone was in the car. She'd plugged it in to charge and forgotten it until now.

Kara debated leaving it but decided the cold wouldn't do the battery any good. So she put on her coat and slipped her boots on. Bracing herself against a wall of frigid air, she held her breath and opened the front door. She trotted across the porch and toward her car, which was already covered with a layer of frost.

She stopped short. Lights were flickering in the windows of Angela's house. At first Kara thought it was the reflection from a streetlight, but as she watched, she saw it again.

Someone was inside.

Curiosity drew her closer. Kara crunched through the snow toward the house. The light seemed to be coming from the back, the kitchen perhaps. Her heart raced as she skirted the house, her heavy breaths forming clouds of white vapor.

The light disappeared.

Maybe she should call the police. But what if she'd imagined the whole thing? She hated to call them out for nothing. And what if they sent Sean? With a firm shake of her head, Kara began trudging back toward the car.

Something—or someone—slammed into her from behind.

Kara went flying forward and landed facedown in the snow.

Sean braked sharply, pulling the cruiser to the curb. Were those lights in Angela's house? He hadn't been aware that anyone was living there. Deciding to check it out without calling in, he grabbed his flashlight and stepped out of the car.

He hadn't planned to drive down this street, since he wasn't supposed to still be on duty. But an impulse had led him here, and now he was glad that it had. Something was afoot.

The light winked off, the windows of the house going blank.

That was strange. Had he imagined seeing it in the first place? Sean stepped off the sidewalk onto the path leading to the house's front door. He turned on the flashlight, using it to sweep the yard and the house.

His beam caught a dark figure running at full speed, hood up and head bowed. "Stop!" he called. "Police!"

The person responded by running faster. Soon footsteps were pounding along the sidewalk away from Sean.

He decided not to pursue and continued toward the house. He would check the doors and windows and figure out how the person had gotten inside.

In the light's beam, Sean saw another figure struggling to get off the ground. Had there been two of them? "Halt!" he shouted. "Police!" In two or three bounds, he covered the ground to the spot.

The person put her hands in front of her face. "Can you move that light? I own this property. Well, my mom does."

Kara? His heart leaped at seeing her twice in one night—after years of barely saying hello. Then his police training kicked in. What was she doing out here in the middle of the night? Had he misinterpreted the entire incident? Maybe Kara and the other person had been inside together.

He shifted the flashlight down. "Sorry. I stopped because I saw a light on in Angela's house. I guess I misread the situation."

"No you didn't," she said. "I saw the light too, and when I came over to investigate, whoever it was knocked me to the ground." She brushed at her pant legs.

Alarm jolted him, and he stepped closer. "Are you okay? You didn't hit your head, did you? Should I call for assistance?"

"I'm fine," Kara said with a laugh. "Couldn't breathe for a few seconds, that's all." She tilted her head. "What are you doing here?"

Sean didn't know how to answer. How could he tell her that some instinct had urged him to make sure that Kara and her mother were all right?

He shuffled his boots in the snow. "I happened to be driving past. Got off shift a little while ago." He waved the beam toward the house. "I was about to see if it's been breached."

"I'm coming with you," she said. "And I think it was. Why else would that person take off? If both of us saw a light, I'm pretty sure we weren't imagining it."

Sean wanted to tell her to go home, that he'd investigate by himself. But he could guess her objection—the house belonged to her mother, so she had a right to check it over. "Come on then. You must be freezing after doing a face-plant in the snow."

His attempt at levity worked, because Kara laughed. "Nothing wakes you up like a face full of cold snow."

Sean checked the front door first, but it was still locked and appeared undamaged, as he had expected. Not many burglars went in through the front, but it was a necessary item on the checklist. Next they went around back, trudging through snow along the side of the house. At each window, he stopped and examined it to make sure it wasn't broken.

As he suspected, they found the evidence at the back door. The storm door was hanging open, and the inner door had been jimmied, the wood around the lock broken.

"I don't suppose you have a security system or cameras?" he asked.

Kara pulled her coat collar up around her neck, seeming to huddle inside the jacket. "No, we never thought we needed them. It's not like we have all kinds of valuables in there. Besides, how many break-ins are there around here?"

Not very many, Sean had to admit. Most of the ones he'd seen happened at plush second homes when the owners were away for months. On this street, houses were close together and neighbors knew one another. Whoever had gotten inside tonight had chosen the time wisely. Not only was it a frigid night, but almost everyone was asleep by now.

"Stay here," Sean said to Kara, using his shoulder to nudge the door open. He didn't think anyone else was in the house, but he wanted to be cautious.

But she followed right on his heels. She reached out and flicked on the light switch, revealing a small mudroom off the kitchen. "What?" she asked in response to his frown. "I used my sleeve." She held her arm up, and the sleeve was pulled down over her fingers.

Deciding not to argue, Sean went farther into the house, listening closely for any sounds. He watched for movement. Nothing. This time he switched on a light.

Behind him, Kara gasped.

Every single cupboard door and drawer was open, their contents spread over the counters and onto the floor. Glass from broken dishes crunched underfoot. Even the fridge door was ajar, although it was empty of everything except a box of baking soda.

"Who did this?" she demanded. "And why? Do you think thieves were looking for something to steal?"

Sean had heard of houses being targeted after their owners died. In this case, though, the owner had been gone for a decade. "I'm not sure, but it's strange timing."

"We keep the bare minimum in here," Kara said. "A set of dishes, some pots and pans, bedding. Our renters are visiting professors, so all they bring are their clothes and laptops." She tried to get past him. "How's the rest of the house?"

"Hold on," he said, moving to block her way. "Let me go first."

"Yes, Mr. Policeman," she muttered, exactly like a sulky child.

Sean hid a smile. Kara had always had a slightly sarcastic wit, a way of puncturing pomposity. She apparently hadn't lost it over the years.

The living room was equally a disaster, with books thrown around and furniture on the floor. The couch cushions had been sliced with a knife.

Kara growled. "I can't believe someone did this to an antique sofa." She rushed to a cushion, her hands outstretched.

"Don't touch anything," Sean warned. "I'm going to get this place dusted." Not that they would be able to pull fingerprints from a fabric surface. He reached for his radio. "In fact, I'm calling this in right now. Why don't you go wait at your house?"

Kara grumbled but finally said, "All right, I'll go." She started toward the kitchen, then halted and faced him again. "Tell me something. What do you think happened to my aunt?"

She got right to the point, another thing he had always admired about her. "She had an accident," he said. "The roads were bad, or something ran out in front of her. I'm sure they'll figure it out in the investigation." He wasn't going to mention the chief's theory that Angela had been impaired.

Kara crossed her arms, regarding him with skepticism. "My aunt went off the road in the exact same spot my dad died. Remember? Now someone has broken into her house and tossed the place. Why? What did they want?"

Sean didn't have any answers. Pressure built up in his temples, exactly as if someone had his head in a vise and was turning the clamp. He knew that Chief Colton preferred simple open-and-shut cases.

But Sean had the distinct feeling that the complexity of Angela Foxworth's death was only beginning to unspool.

As Kara opened the front door and slipped inside, her mother called from upstairs. "Kara, is that you?"

Kara sighed. She'd been hoping that her mother would sleep through this whole thing.

"It's me. I forgot my phone in the car." In fact, she had barely remembered to grab it on the way inside.

To her chagrin, her mother appeared at the top of the stairs, wearing a fuzzy robe over her nightgown. "I can't sleep."

Kara gritted her teeth. She would have preferred to tell her mother about the ransacked house in the bright light of day. Her plan had been to wait in the living room until the police came to get her statement, which she would give sitting in one of their warm vehicles. That wasn't an option anymore.

"You had better come downstairs," Kara said. "There's something I need to tell you."

Clearly alarmed, her mother hurried down the steps, gripping the polished banister firmly with her right hand. "What is it?" she asked when she reached the bottom.

Kara slipped her hand through her mother's arm. "Come sit in the living room." She guided her across the hall and over to the sofa.

Her mom obeyed, staring at her with wide, frightened eyes. She played with the sash of her robe, threading it through her fingers over and over.

Kara perched beside her. "Someone broke into Aunt Angela's

house tonight." She took her mother through the whole incident, how she'd accidentally spotted the light on and how the intruder had practically run her over. The fortunate appearance of Sean Colton and what they had discovered.

"The police are going to take prints to see if they can find any evidence of who did this," Kara explained. "I told Sean that I had no idea why anyone would bother to search Angela's house. There's nothing of value there, right?"

"No, we cleaned out the house before we let anyone rent it. I have everything of value that she owned, or it's at the bank in a safe-deposit box."

Kara thought of something. "Did Angela have a will?"

"Yes, she did. You and I are her beneficiaries. Walter Hill, the attorney she used to work for, will probably want to meet with us." Her mother reached for a tissue and dabbed at her eyes. "Since we're in Vermont, I could have had her declared dead after five years, but I never wanted to do that."

"I don't blame you," Kara said. That would have meant accepting that Angela would never return home. Now they were being forced to do just that. "If she didn't have anything of great value and no one else benefits from her will, then why did someone break in?"

"We might never know," her mom said with a sigh. She glanced at the mantel clock. "I'm exhausted. But do you want me to stay up with you?"

"No, I'm fine." Kara slouched into a more comfortable position. "I'll make a pot of coffee. Go back to bed. I'll give you the update in the morning."

Her mother bent over and hugged her. "See you in the morning. Pancakes and bacon?" It was one of Kara's favorite breakfast meals.

"Absolutely," Kara said, hoisting herself off the couch. Before going to the kitchen, she went to the front window and peeked outside.

Three cruisers were parked at Angela's house, blue lights flashing. She yawned. Hopefully they wouldn't take too long to come talk to her.

She padded into the kitchen, where she made a pot of coffee. When she checked the pink hippopotamus cookie jar she'd always loved, she hit the jackpot. It was full to the brim with chocolate chip, toffee chip, and oatmeal cookies. She pulled out a selection and arranged them on a plate. She set mugs, spoons, and napkins on the vintage Formica table, then added the cookies, a sugar bowl, and a small carton of half-and-half.

Once the coffee finished brewing, she poured a partial cup, not wanting to be awake all night. She nabbed a chocolate chip cookie and went to the living room to wait.

Kara checked her phone, finding nothing new in her in-box or on social media. With her pulse pounding, she checked the local news page.

There it was. *Hiker Discovers Missing Woman's Vehicle.* Heart in her throat, she scanned the short write-up. They'd found remains in the vehicle, but identification hadn't been confirmed.

Kara bit back hysterical laughter. They didn't need any more confirmation. Everyone knew who it was in that car. But she supposed they were obliged to go through official channels. Or at least give lip service to that process.

Someone rapped on the front door, followed by the murmur of voices.

Putting down her phone, Kara hurried to answer. Sean and Chief Colton were standing on the porch. "Thanks for not ringing the bell," she said, standing back to let them enter. "My mother is in bed."

"We won't take long," the chief assured her.

"I made coffee," Kara said. "It's in the kitchen."

Chief Colton rubbed his hands together. "Coffee sounds great. It's shaping up to be a cold one out there tonight. Below zero, they said."

Kara settled them at the table with full mugs, then sat at one end. The two police officers faced each other across the middle.

Spoons clanked as they added half-and-half and sugar.

Chief Colton nodded at Sean, who pulled out a tablet to take notes.

Earlier he'd been like the old Sean—her friend. Who was this grim, quiet man in uniform? Then he sent her a covert smile, and she relaxed. He was probably just trying to remain professional.

"All right, take us through tonight," the chief said to Kara. "Tell us what happened at your aunt's house."

"I don't know," she said. "My mother had gone to bed, and I went out to my car to get my cell phone. I saw lights on in Angela's house." Chief Colton sipped from his mug. "Did you go inside?"

"No, not until I went in with Officer Colton," Kara answered.

"So you didn't go inside before Officer Colton arrived," the chief said, sounding skeptical. "Do you and your mother have a key to Angela's place?"

Kara tensed at the chief's tone of voice and the direction of his questioning. Did he actually think *she* had vandalized Angela's home? Why would she do that? Her mother owned the place. Kara had the right to be there and no motive to ransack it.

"We sure do," Kara said, pointing to a rack of hooks by the back door, where several sets of keys hung. "Want me to get it?"

"Not right now," Chief Colton said, waving his hand. "Was anything missing?" He picked up a cookie and dunked it into his coffee.

Kara ran a hand through her hair. "I don't know. I didn't spend much time in there. I'd have to go through the place more closely to figure that out. But we didn't keep anything valuable at Aunt Angela's anyway. We have renters now and then."

"About the other person, the one who ran away." Chief Colton abruptly changed gears. "Who was it?"

Again Kara felt his suspicion. Did he honestly think she'd ransacked the place with an accomplice, then played dumb when Sean showed up?

She lifted her chin in defiance. "I have no idea who it was. I don't even know if it was a man or a woman. I never saw the person's face. When I went out to get my phone, I saw a light on in the house. I went to investigate, the light went out, and someone knocked me down." She glanced at Sean, diligently taking notes. "You saw the whole thing. Tell him."

"He saw someone running away," the chief said. "He told me that he didn't even know you were there until he stumbled over you."

Kara's cheeks heated. Was Sean actually going along with the chief's line of questioning? And why did that idea sting like a betrayal? "Yes, because I had been knocked off my feet and into the snow. I wasn't spending time on the ground because I enjoy it."

"Maybe you fell," Chief Colton suggested.

"No, I didn't fall," she objected.

"It's my job to ask tough questions. You understand?" The chief gave her a reassuring pat on the hand. "We can see that your aunt's house was trashed by someone, so we took prints. We might not get anything useful from them, especially if you've had renters. But why don't you and your mother come by the station and we'll take your fingerprints for comparison purposes?"

Kara understood the logic of that, but resistance to the directive rose up in her core. She couldn't help but feel that the chief would use their prints to frame them as the vandals. Surely almost everyone was smart enough to wear gloves when conducting a crime nowadays. Then she bit back a laugh at how ridiculous she was being, probably due to lack of sleep. The chief was gruff, but she'd never known him to be anything but fair.

She thought of something. "I want a copy of the police report.

In case we do discover something valuable missing. We'll need it for the insurance company."

Chief Colton raised his brows as if surprised that she was savvy enough to make this request. "Of course. When you come by the station, we can give you a copy."

Kara nodded.

Chief Colton ate the rest of his cookie, watching her all the while. "If there's anything else you want to tell us about this incident, feel free to give me a call." He reached into his breast pocket and pulled out a card, which he placed on the table. "My direct line is right there. We know this is a rough time for you and your mother, and the department is here for you."

"Thank you," Kara said numbly, going through the motions of being polite.

She stared at the two officers, the chief drinking his coffee, Sean still taking notes, and suddenly felt very much alone. Whatever the truth was concerning her aunt's death, she wasn't confident that these two men would help her uncover it. Neither one had even mentioned the profound coincidence that Angela's body had been found and her home had been broken into on the same night.

No, Kara was certain that she and her mother were on their own.

The chief carefully made his way to Sean's side, so as not to slip on the icy ground.

Sean braced himself. He had the cruiser door open, ready to get in and go home. The third cruiser was gone from Angela's house, those officers having been charged with collecting fingerprint samples.

"What made you come down this street?" Despite the dim light from the streetlight, Chief Colton's gaze burned into his face.

Sean shrugged. "I wanted to check out Angela's house. Good thing I did, right?" He tossed his messenger bag inside the car. He certainly wasn't going to admit wanting to make sure Kara and her mother were okay.

The chief stepped closer. "Please don't tell me it was because of Kara."

His uncle had never thought much of Kara for some reason, and Sean had never understood that. Kara was a nice person, a good student, and a talented athlete. What wasn't to like? But the whole time Sean had dated her, his uncle had expressed a distinct lack of enthusiasm. Not that it had mattered, since Sean's parents had liked her. But they were a thousand miles away now, and the chief was right here.

"I was worried," Sean said. "I mean, we just pulled her aunt out of the woods. What if Kara or her mother is next?" Even as he said it, he heard how lame it sounded. He had no reason to think they were in danger. But on the other hand, someone *had* broken into Angela's place. So it was a good thing he'd been in the vicinity.

The chief fisted his hands on his hips. "Next for what? You know it was an accident, plain and simple. Angela was probably driving too fast and went off the road. It happened to her brother too, remember?"

"How could I forget?" Sean gritted out, recalling that he had indeed forgotten the details of Miles Foxworth's car accident until Kara reminded him.

Chief Colton rested a heavy hand on Sean's shoulder. "Go home and get some sleep. See you in the morning."

Sean wanted to ask when the chief thought the forensic reports would come in, but he didn't bother bringing it up. The last thing he wanted was for the chief to make good on his earlier threat and shut Sean out of the case. Besides, his interest didn't really have anything to do with Kara. He wanted to learn the truth about what had happened to Angela, as he would for any citizen of Castlebridge who had met an untimely demise. Yes, that was his motive.

The chief strode to his cruiser and drove away.

As Sean climbed into the car, he noticed a light was on upstairs in Kara's house. While he watched, it winked out.

He was lying to himself. Maybe he'd managed to suppress his feelings for years, but he still cared about Kara. A lot.

As memories of their time together floated through his tired mind, Sean drove home through quiet side streets decorated for Christmas. He enjoyed the Nativity scenes the most. *The reason for the season, right?*

His apartment was over the garage of a stately old mansion owned by an elderly landlady he adored. It didn't take one of Sean's psychology classes to inform him that Miss Eleanor had become a mother figure—even if she was his grandparents' age—much the way the chief had acted as a father figure after his parents moved away.

Sean pulled into the drive and parked beside the garage side entrance. The rules of their small force meant they were allowed to take cruisers home. Residents liked the deterrent of seeing cruisers in their neighborhoods, especially this area, which had many elderly homeowners.

Still thinking about Kara, Sean gathered his bag and climbed out of the cruiser. He was exhausted. All the turmoil and stress of the car retrieval followed by the adrenaline rush of the break-in had wiped him out. His gait was lumbering as he unlocked the door and entered the garage. The stairs to his apartment were straight ahead, and he had to use the banister to help climb the flight. Hopefully tomorrow would bring fresh energy—and more answers. Kara and her mother deserved them.

A pounding of paws greeted the scratch of the key in the lock. By the time Sean got the door open, his rescue tiger cat, Bandit, was already wailing as if he'd been abandoned for days. Still an adolescent, the cat had massive paws, a big head, and huge green eyes. One ear was ragged on the edge, a trophy from a previous fight, no doubt.

More than one person had teased Sean about a cop owning a cat named Bandit. But the name was a natural after Sean had caught him stealing his turkey sandwich. Sean had left it on the patio table while he raked the yard for Miss Eleanor.

After asking around the neighborhood and calling shelters, Sean figured out the cat was a stray and, at Miss Eleanor's urging, adopted him. At age eighty-five, his landlady was too old to take care of a cat, and her housekeeper refused to. So that was that.

"I know, buddy." Sean bent to pat the cat. "It was a long day. And not a very good one."

Bandit meowed.

Sean replenished the cat's food and water, then unhooked his duty belt. The gun he put away securely, according to regulations.

After washing up and getting ready for bed, he gathered Bandit into his arms and sat in the rocking chair by the window. Here, as was his ritual, he read a Bible passage and prayed, allowing the burdens of the day to seep away.

Now, more than any other time in his career, Sean needed strength and fresh resolve to face the challenges ahead.

"Good morning," Rhonda Peabody said. The secretary at the station, a middle-aged woman with dyed jet-black hair and thickly penciled brows, was a marvel of efficiency and organization. Seated in a rolling chair, she moved from her desk along a file credenza and drawers, where she deposited one stack of papers and retrieved another.

Sean greeted her.

"Heard you had quite a lot of excitement last night." Rhonda frowned. "On top of..." Blinking, she shook her head and whispered, "I can't believe it."

Sean fiddled with the zipper of his jacket, his thoughts consumed by the memory of Angela's mangled car crawling up that hillside through the woods like an approaching nightmare.

"Me neither," he finally said. He didn't trust himself to say anything else to the motherly Rhonda, because that would release all the sorrow and confusion he felt and give voice to the questions that demanded answers.

Although Sean wasn't officially on duty until later, he'd come by the station to hear any updates. He was eager to dig in and solve the mystery of Angela's death.

Rhonda swiveled back and forth in her chair a few times, making it squeak. Then she glanced over her shoulder and leaned forward. "I never believed the rumors."

Sean raised a hand. "Please don't." The chief had a rule about gossip, although that didn't stop the officers and other staff from indulging behind his back. But Sean could hear his uncle talking in his office across the big room to somebody.

Despite his warning, Rhonda continued. "Everyone said she ran off with a man, but I never believed it." Spots of color flamed in her powdered cheeks. "Why would she when she and that wonderful Nelson Reed were an item? They were inseparable. I was sure he was going to pop the question. Then she was gone."

Sean had been a teenager at the time, so he hadn't paid attention to Angela's—or any adult's—dating life. Now he could see why Angela and Nelson had been together. Both had a good sense of humor, and they were intelligent and hardworking. Surprisingly, Nelson, who owned a dairy farm outside town, remained single. Still carrying a torch for Angela after all these years? The thought made Sean's heart hurt. For Nelson, he told himself. Not because he could relate.

But on the flip side, as Angela's known significant other, suspicion would definitely fall on Nelson if foul play was determined. Police always investigated partners, friends, and family first. Sean wondered if Chief Colton planned to talk to Nelson. If so, he'd love to sit in on the interview.

Sean leaned against a nearby desk. "Do you think Angela would have said yes?"

"In a heartbeat," Rhonda replied, the squeak of her chair echoing her excitement. "Anytime you saw them together, you couldn't help but think, 'There's a couple in love.'"

Had Sean and Kara ever inspired such thoughts in passersby? Glad that Rhonda couldn't read his mind, he quickly shut down that line of thought. "But people thought she ran off with someone else?"

"You know how it is around here. Someone speculates, and by the time it goes a block, it's a verified fact." She bit her bottom lip. "Funny thing is, no one could ever give his name or a description."

"It'd have to be a pretty powerful love for her to abandon her family, job, and home," Sean said. How hard had anyone tried to find her? When he thought that all these years, she'd been lying there undiscovered, alone in a woodland grave . . .

He took a deep breath, trying to control the anger and sadness roiling in his midsection.

"I agree with you," Rhonda said. "I never believed it. But there wasn't any sign of foul play and certainly not—" She stopped short, but Sean heard the words as plainly as if she had said them. *A body.*

"How did Nelson take it?" Sean asked. "Do you recall?" He knew he was veering into interrogation territory, but he felt compelled to learn as much as he could. Whatever was going on in Angela's life might have had bearing on her death. Even if it was as simple as she was upset about something and that contributed to the accident.

"He was naturally devastated," Rhonda answered. "He told anyone who would listen that she hadn't run off. After a while he gave up on that, since folks started to avoid him. He's more or less kept to himself ever since." She cocked her head. "Well, he was always sort of a loner, so busy with his farm, you know. But he and Angela used to go to cultural events and eat out quite a bit. I rarely see him now."

If anyone would run into Nelson, it was Rhonda. She was the busiest bee Sean had ever met, with a finger in every organization, event, and civic affair in Castlebridge.

Ryan put his head around the doorjamb of the chief's office. "Hey, Colton. The chief wants to see you." As usual, he wore a smile that skated on the knife's edge of outright mockery.

"Duty calls," Sean told Rhonda. "Talk to you later." He took off his coat and hung it on a peg, then headed for the chief's office.

As he reached the doorway, Ryan emerged, making sure to bump shoulders with him as they crossed paths. Sean shook his head but didn't rise to the bait.

Chief Colton was typing on his computer, glasses perched partway down his nose. "Morning. Have a seat."

Sean obeyed. "How are you this morning?"

His uncle grunted a response, not lifting his eyes from the screen. "Just a minute." He punched a few buttons on the keyboard, and papers began to spit out of the printer. Once they were done, he gathered them up and slid them onto the desk in front of Sean. "That's the preliminary report on the Foxworth case. We'll have more later today." He clasped his hands together and watched as Sean picked up the pages.

At first Sean thought the chief was referring to the break-in and this was a report on the fingerprinting, but then he saw the name on top. *Jane Doe.* They wouldn't correct that until identity had been firmly established. "Can they get dental records?" he asked.

"Yes, I believe so. They're calling around to the local dentists this morning on the presumption that it's Angela." The chief picked up his mug and slurped coffee.

Sean skimmed the page, doing his best to concentrate on what he was reading. The report gave a description of what the officers had found—details of the car and its location, the damage it had sustained, and the position of the occupant as well as the belongings inside.

In the blur of all he was trying to absorb, one fact stood out as if highlighted in neon. *Seat belt restraint was not fastened.*

Why had Angela—conscientious, law-abiding Angela—been driving without her seat belt?

The aroma of bacon, coffee, and pancakes enticed Kara from her bed. Her eyes barely open, she glanced at the clock while tying on a robe. *Yikes.* It was later than she'd thought. She pushed her feet into soft old slippers and shuffled downstairs.

"Morning, sunshine," her mother greeted her. She slid the spatula under a pancake and flipped it to reveal a perfect golden-brown crust. "I thought the smell of breakfast might lure you out of your lair."

This was a long-standing joke between them. Kara was a night owl, and her mother had battled to wake her all through her childhood. Kara still liked to sleep in when she could, but this morning it had been totally unplanned.

Kara went to the coffee maker and poured a cup. "I'm glad I didn't miss you. What time do you have to be at the library?"

"Nine. But you know me—I don't like to rush in the morning."

Yawning, Kara sat down at the table. She poured cream into her cup and stirred, then took that first delightful sip. "You make the best coffee."

Busy at the stove, her mom said absently, "Thanks, hon." She put three pancakes in a stack, added a couple of bacon strips, and set the plate on the table. "This afternoon we have an appointment at Walter Hill's office."

Kara's hand stilled on the butter knife. "The will?"

"That's right. He wants to go over the papers with us." Her mother filled her own cup and sat down in the same chair Sean had chosen the night before.

"Aren't you eating?" Kara swirled the butter around until it melted, then poured a generous pool of maple syrup onto the pancakes. This jug was from the Reed Farm, according to the label. Her mom liked to support local farmers.

"I already had something." Her mother smiled. "An hour ago."

"All right, rub it in." Kara laughed. "I'm a slacker."

Her mom sipped coffee. "Well, you are on vacation. Think you can keep yourself busy this morning?"

Kara had already decided how she would spend the morning—next door, searching Aunt Angela's house. If there was anything there that could shed light on her aunt's life before she disappeared, Kara wanted to find it.

But all she said to her mother was, "I'll just hang around and relax." She cut a big forkful of pancake and added a bit of bacon. The combination was heavenly. "What time should we meet?"

Her mother tapped the table with a forefinger. "I have an idea. Want to go to lunch at Upper Crust before the appointment?"

Kara paused in the act of taking another bite. "You don't have to ask me twice. A big yes on that one." Upper Crust served wonderful soups and delectable sandwiches on homemade bread. She and her mother made a point of eating there every time Kara visited.

Her mom drank the last of her coffee. "Why don't you come by the library and pick me up? No sense in taking two cars."

"Sounds like a plan," Kara said.

Both she and her mother were obviously avoiding a discussion of the previous night's events. This was not the time to get into it, not with her mother needing to go to work. Another person might call in sick and wallow but not her mom. She often said the structure of her days held her up when events threatened to knock her over.

Then Kara remembered the chief's request and knew she had to mention it. "We have one more thing we need to do this afternoon. The chief wants to take our prints to eliminate them from the ones they took last night."

Her mother sighed. "I suppose we'd better get it over with, though I doubt it will help. I didn't have a chance to do a deep cleaning after the last tenant so I'm sure there are tons of fingerprints."

"They probably wore gloves too," Kara said glumly. "Everyone knows you should when you break into a place."

"That's what I've gleaned from watching television." Her mom pushed back in her chair. "I'd better get going."

"I'll clean up," Kara offered.

"Thanks," her mother said, then went upstairs to finish getting ready.

Kara poured a refill of coffee and grabbed another bacon slice. As she made her way back to her seat, she brushed against some mail stacked on the counter. A magazine slid and several letters fell to the floor.

As she picked up the usual assortment of bills, one business-size envelope stood out. The paper was thick and creamy, and she was surprised by the return address. It was from Fuller Property Partners. The company was owned by Benedict Fuller, a prominent citizen and one of the wealthiest people in town. More than a hundred years ago, his family had built the redbrick textile mill complex that still dominated part of downtown. It was currently being redeveloped to house a variety of businesses, even some apartments.

Benedict Fuller obviously had influence in town. His opinion was sought out regarding issues big and small. He was the man everyone wanted on their guest list, the first to be approached during a fundraising campaign. Some people said—often with an undertone of resentment—that he ran the town.

Kara didn't trust him one bit. His company had been buying

properties in neglected pockets of town and replacing them with much more expensive homes. Gentrification, they called it.

What in the world did he want with her mother? Kara stared at the envelope, her conscience warring. Curiosity won out after she decided on a compromise. She'd peek at the letter and tell her mother she had when they got together for lunch. And she'd apologize for being nosy.

Kara unfolded the single sheet of paper. Holding her breath, she scanned the printed words, then noted the large, arrogant scrawl of a signature. *Benedict.*

He wanted to buy both Foxworth homes. Terms to be discussed.

After reading the letter, Kara couldn't sit and enjoy another cup of coffee. Instead, as the letter played through her mind again and again, she cleaned the kitchen and got ready for the day.

As a counterpoint to her dismay, she told herself that it was her mother's decision to sell or not. There really wasn't any reason to keep the homes, except for all the memories they held. Her mother could live somewhere newer, with easier maintenance.

Why then was Kara's gut reaction a definite no? Because her whole childhood was bound up in this home? Because she couldn't imagine visiting her mother anywhere else? That was rather selfish.

Kara still hadn't come to any resolution by the time she slipped out the back door, crossed a small deck, and descended into the snowy yard. The day was cold and still, with thin clouds trailing across a blue sky. Birds twittered and chirped around feeders on the deck, scattering seed hulls everywhere, and a lone car drove slowly up the street.

At this time of day, everyone was at work or school, or if retired, still warmly inside. The temperature was too cold for a casual walk. At other times of year, there was almost always someone out and about in the neighborhood. It was one reason Kara liked it so much. It was a friendly place, where people watched out for one another.

Kara began to tromp through ankle-deep snow toward Angela's house. Instead of cutting across the driveway, she went around the garage and accessed the door that way. For some reason it seemed important that people not know she was inside.

The traces of black fingerprint powder smudged on the back door reminded her why she was being so cautious. Someone out there was worried enough about something to break into Angela's home and tear it apart, searching the place.

But why now? Angela had been gone for ten years, which had been ample time for someone to do this.

A memory niggled. Right after Angela's disappearance, her mother had asked Kara if she'd been in the house, since she'd found the door unlocked. Kara hadn't. At that point, she couldn't even bring herself to go inside. Her mother chalked it up to her own poor memory but changed the locks anyway.

Then she had another revelation. The police and emergency personnel were first on the accident scene, which meant they'd had a prime opportunity to search Angela's car. Her heart twisted. *Sean.* Could she trust him?

The dismay she felt at this thought revealed something stunning. She *wanted* to trust him—even though he'd proven once that she couldn't. After dating for a couple of years, he had dumped her for another girl, shattering her heart. But they had been kids then. Couldn't she forgive him for a youthful indiscretion?

She'd have to think about that.

Shaking her head, Kara opened the door, stepped into the kitchen, and listened. A little late, she wondered if someone else was inside. "Is anyone here?" she called before she thought better of it.

Nothing answered except the hum of the furnace switching on in the basement.

She took another tentative step forward, wincing at the kitchen's disarray and the black smudges everywhere. She questioned if they really needed to use so much of that powder.

Keeping her gloves on, Kara moved slowly through the rooms. She picked up books off the floor and leafed through those still standing on shelves. She stacked slashed cushions in a heap to be either repaired or replaced. She swept up glass from broken dishes and picture frames and dumped it all into the trash can, the glass hitting the bottom and breaking into even smaller shards. One piece of artwork she found on the floor was a large embroidered view of a covered bridge. Kara thought Angela had done it herself, so she set it aside to take home.

She'd do her best to keep her mother out of here until she got it cleaned up. Seeing this mess would only upset her more. Maybe Kara could hire someone to help, since a thorough cleaning of this home had not been on her vacation agenda.

Neither had the discovery that her aunt was truly gone.

A sob pushed its way up into Kara's chest, erupting in a great hiccup of grief. *Aunt Angela.* Now that hope was totally destroyed, Kara realized how much she'd hoped to see her aunt again. That she would write or call or simply show up on their doorstep. It wasn't like Angela to disappear, but Kara had imagined wild reasons. Perhaps she'd been in witness protection. Or she'd been working undercover for the government.

Anything besides crashing her car and remaining undiscovered for a decade.

Kara found tissues in the bathroom and used one to dry her eyes. She'd been through a major loss once, and she knew the grief would come and go. It was important to allow the roller coaster, not try to suppress it. Gradually, finally, the painful bouts would lessen, and deep, wrenching sorrow would be replaced by a gentler sadness. She and her mother could talk about her father now, and they often shared special memories, especially those that made them laugh. He would have liked that. Her father had encouraged her to feel her emotions but also to release them once they had served their purpose.

Kara continued her task. Her belly tightened as she approached Angela's room. They'd cleaned it of personal items after it became clear that Angela wasn't returning anytime soon, but Kara still felt intrusive whenever she entered.

The room wasn't overly large, but it was spacious enough to hold a lovely walnut bedroom suite, including a couple of dressers. With windows on two walls, sunlight streamed in, gleaming on satiny hardwood floors and matching woodwork.

The intruder had contented himself with pulling out the dresser drawers and throwing them down. Hoping they weren't damaged, Kara picked them up and slid them back into their slots. She discovered only a ding or two, nothing that couldn't be fixed with some polish.

Next she searched the closet, using a chair to reach the top shelf. Under the shelf paper, unchanged since Angela's disappearance, she discovered a birthday card from Nelson to Angela, signed, "All my love." He had included the date—her birthday the year she disappeared.

Kara studied the card as if it held clues to the relationship between her aunt and the farmer. The sentiment, while not gushing, definitely meant more than friendship. How serious had the couple been? Kara thought of one way she could find out.

She would pay Nelson Reed a visit as soon as possible.

8

The discovery of the birthday card energized Kara. Here was something, maybe a clue to Aunt Angela's life before she died. She decided to show the card to Nelson when she visited him. She also took the beautiful covered bridge embroidery, not wanting to leave it for possible vandals.

And that thought was a reminder. They should get a locksmith over here to change the locks and install a security system. Maybe it was a case of shutting the barn door after the horse was stolen, but Kara didn't want to take any chances.

Back at the house, Kara changed into light wool slacks, a matching sweater, and leather ankle boots. She wanted to put her best foot forward when she and her mother met with the attorney, and she wanted to look nice for their lunch date.

A short while later, she was in her car and headed along the familiar route to the college library. Rather than go downtown, she circled through the neighborhoods, realizing how close they lived to the college. Was that why Benedict Fuller wanted their house? For a project related to the school? It seemed that over the past few decades the college had continued to expand, becoming more and more of an economic hub for the area. It wasn't a bad thing in itself, but it was bound to bring changes to the historic town.

Since most of the college, other than the library, was closed for the holidays, Kara easily found an open parking spot in the library visitor lot. The brick-and-glass building was new, but the architects had designed it to fit in with the older buildings.

She ascended wide granite steps, nodding greetings to others coming and going. Inside the double doors, she had a choice of the elevator or stairs to the main floor. She chose the stairs.

Her mother was working at the long desk straight across from the entrance. She smiled when she saw her daughter. "Hey, you're early," she said with a laugh. "Everything okay?"

"Fine," Kara said, unwinding her scarf. "I thought I'd do some browsing before lunch." She didn't tell her mother the real plan—to search the newspaper archives for articles about her father and aunt. Maybe she could discover some clues that she hadn't picked up on in the past.

"Do you need my help finding anything?" her mom asked.

Kara grinned. "No, I think I know my way around. I've been coming here since before I could read." That was how long her mother had been a librarian, back when they were in the old, cramped library before this new one was built. But the organization of materials was the same, although sleek banks of computer monitors had replaced clunky older models.

Thinking of Angela's house, she stepped closer to the desk and lowered her voice. "You need to call a locksmith. I think we should change the locks next door and even put in a security system. They don't cost much nowadays."

Her mother's smile faltered. "You really think so? I mean, it was probably kids or someone trying to take advantage of an empty house."

Kara didn't believe that in the least. "Well, even so, they don't need to be messing around in there. We'll be liable if someone gets hurt."

"That's true." Her mom reached for her cell phone. "I'll call right now."

"I'll be lost in the archives," Kara said. "Meet you here at noon?"

Her mother nodded.

With a wave, Kara headed toward the reference section. The first task was to log on and find out exactly what newspapers and publications the library carried. At a college, the selection should be good.

On her way across the room, Kara saw a portly older man bustling toward her. Dressed in a fine gray wool suit, he was bald, with a beaky nose and an air of importance. Everett Douglas, the college president. His gaze skittered over her, returned, then skated away.

Something about that annoyed Kara. Maybe he didn't recognize her—there were easily a thousand young women who worked and studied at the college. But he hadn't even attempted to acknowledge her. And had he *really* not recognized her? Kara had met the college president dozens of times over the years, and she'd been told that she was the spitting image of her mother. Considering the fact that she and her mother had just suffered a grievous loss, his discourtesy was a slap in the face.

A stubborn whim made her stop right in front of him, feet planted wide. "Good morning, President Douglas. How are you today?" Her voice rang out clear and true, and those nearby whipped their heads toward the conversation. "Kara Foxworth. Michelle Foxworth's daughter."

He was forced to stop, both by her position and the attention of others. "Good morning, Ms. Foxworth. I didn't know you were in town."

Kara folded her arms. "I certainly am. For the holidays." She tilted her head, wondering if she should say anything about Angela. Why not? "I'm sure you've heard the sad news."

"Sad news?" Everett repeated. He seemed confused. "I'm not—"

"My aunt," Kara said. "Her body was found yesterday." In the genteel surroundings of the library, her words sounded loud and harsh.

He took a step back, his hand going to his necktie. "Oh yes. I was so very sorry to hear about her accident. My condolences to you and your mother."

Surprised by her own boldness, Kara moved forward. Something about Everett Douglas and his smugness was irritating her right now, even more than usual. "What's really upsetting to me is that no one took us seriously when she disappeared." *Including you.*

Her mother had hoped that her boss and the head of the largest institution in town would sway the police into trying harder—or at all. But they'd all dismissed the situation. And the whole time Angela was only a couple of miles away.

Apparently flummoxed by her remark, Everett ran a manicured hand over his bald head, as though to smooth nonexistent hair. "There was absolutely no indication that anything had happened. Surely we would have tried . . ." His voice trailed off, and he reached forward as though to pat her shoulder,

Kara evaded his touch.

"I'm sure it's all very upsetting and understandably so. My best to you and your mother." With that, the man began moving again.

Kara watched him go, relieved when he didn't stop at the desk to talk to her mom. She hadn't thought about the potential repercussions for her mother before confronting her boss. Her mom loved her work, and she was good at it. She had even been voted favorite librarian more than once. She'd be devastated to lose her job, and Kara would feel awful if she were the cause.

Kara found an empty computer station and sat, then wiggled the mouse to light up the screen. All she could do was keep moving and find some answers.

This computer gave her access to the library catalog, including physical and digital books, publications, and databases. Kara wanted the local newspapers. After a brief search, she discovered that back issues were housed downstairs in the archives. More recent issues were digitized, but the years Kara wanted were still on microfilm.

Making a note of where she could find the right film, Kara gathered her belongings and headed for the closest stairwell door. Down she went, boots clattering on the concrete steps. At the bottom, a door opened into a corridor lined with doors.

Initially when she stepped through, the hallway was disconcertingly dark. But then the overhead lights flickered and came on, triggered by a motion detector, likely installed to save energy. As she moved down the hall in search of the publications archive, the lights glowed for a moment and then darkened behind her.

It was located at the very end. This room was sizable, lined with shelves holding boxes and bound newspapers. She wanted to browse through newspapers from a hundred years ago, enjoying the quaint ads and glimpses of life they provided. But she didn't have time for that right now. Since the room was stuffy, she left the door open to the hall.

In a bank of filing cabinets along the wall, Kara found the *Castlebridge Gazette*. After a little more searching, she found the correct years and extracted the boxes. Then she loaded the microfilm onto a reel, fondly remembering learning to do so under her mother's gentle instruction.

As she scanned the issues, her heart lurched when she noticed a headline. *One Dead in Car Crash*. She had to close her eyes against the words as unhappy memories and raw emotions flooded her body in a sickening wave. She clasped her hands so tightly that her fingernails left marks on her skin.

Breathe. After a moment, Kara recovered enough composure to read the article. It was short, without many details. Miles Foxworth, 47, local architect, had lost control of his car on the so-called Dead Man's Curve and hit a tree. Death was believed to have been instantaneous.

Thank God for small mercies. At least her father hadn't suffered. As Kara absorbed this bare-bones account, she realized what was missing. There was no mention of bad road conditions, another vehicle, or even an implication that her dad had been impaired. Which he hadn't been, of course. He never drank alcohol, and he wasn't on any medications. He always wore his seat belt, and he never used his cell phone while driving. No, her father had been a very safe and healthy man.

So what had caused him to go off the road?

Rather than print the article, Kara took a picture with her phone. Pages printed at the front desk, and she didn't want anyone to know what she was researching. Not even her mother, who didn't need the shock of seeing this article unexpectedly.

There wasn't much else about her father after that one article. An obituary, yes, which mentioned his respected work in Castlebridge. His firm had worked on the Fuller Mill revitalization plans and various projects for the college. She wondered what he would have thought of Benedict Fuller trying to buy his home. Probably not much, since he had been fiercely independent and not easily impressed by status or wealth. He'd taught Kara to focus on people's merit, not their public images.

The lights flickered overhead.

Kara moved her arms, thinking she'd been sitting too still and not wanting the lights to time out.

Heavy footsteps echoed out in the hall. She expected them to stop at one of the other rooms, but they kept coming. Steady and relentless. *Thump, thump, thump.*

The hair stood up on the back of Kara's neck even as she told herself she was being ridiculous. It had to be a student who hadn't gone home for the holidays or a faculty member doing research.

The lights went out. And they didn't come back on.

Sean set his pen down on the table with a sigh. After leaving the police station, he'd come to the college library to do some research, although officially he was on Christmas break from his classes. But as an adult student with a full-time job, he needed to work ahead as much as possible.

He'd learned this lesson the hard way during his first semester when mandatory overtime had put a crimp in his studying. Today it was the Angela Foxworth case interfering with his concentration. After reading and taking notes for an hour, he'd had to admit that nothing was sinking in, no matter how many times he reread the same information.

Sean leaned back in his chair and stared out the narrow window at a view of bare tree branches and blue sky. He was alone up here, a real change from the end of the semester when all the students suffering from procrastination and panic had mobbed the library to work on papers and study for exams.

His mood today was unusual. Reading about criminal psychology always fascinated him to the point that he often had five or six texts stacked on the desk. As he read, he tried to apply the theories to real-life cases in Castlebridge. The more he understood about the way criminals thought, the more he would be able to uncover past actions and predict future behavior.

As a detective for the state police, he would be able to help make Vermont a safer place for its citizens. As it stood now, the Castlebridge municipal force handled minor crimes, managed traffic, and enforced local ordinances. The duties were important, but Sean couldn't exactly sink his teeth into any of them.

To Sean's mind, the fact that Angela Foxworth hadn't been wearing a seat belt stood out like a neon sign. But he was the only one who appeared to see it. When he'd raised the point, Chief Colton had brushed him off.

"It doesn't mean a thing," the chief said. "So she forgot to buckle up. Not that it would have saved her life if she had. No, the impact of the crash was fatal." He sounded so sure of himself.

Judging by the distance the car had traveled down the slope and the impact with a large pine before falling over the ravine cliff, his uncle was probably right. But still, the seat belt issue raised doubts in Sean's mind. He was sure it meant something. But what?

He would continue to keep an open mind and review the evidence. If something indicated foul play rather than an accident, he would talk to the state police. Maybe without the chief's knowledge if he still wasn't receptive. Sean would hate to do that. But how many cases had been solved because someone refused to accept evidence at face value and kept digging until the truth came to light?

Sean wanted to count himself among those who fought for justice, who took the risk of bucking the status quo.

With a grunt of derision at his own hubris, Sean pushed back from the table. He obviously wasn't going to get any studying done today. He'd check out the books and try again after lunch. Or tomorrow.

After putting his notebook, tablet, and pen into his bag, he gathered the armload of books and headed for the stairwell.

On the main floor, he approached the front desk, where Michelle Foxworth was working.

She motioned to his books and smiled. "The semester is over. Didn't you get the memo?"

With a laugh, he set the books on the counter. "I'm getting a head start on my next classes. Got to make the most of the break."

"I wish more students thought like you," Michelle said as she checked out the books. "But I guess it's human nature to put things off."

"It totally is," Sean agreed. The big clock on the wall said it was almost noon, and his stomach rumbled. "Sorry. I guess it's lunchtime."

Michelle glanced at the clock, a furrow appearing between her brows. "It sure is. I wonder where Kara is."

Sean noticed that his heart leaped at the sound of her name. *How ridiculous is that?* "Is she meeting you here?"

"She's supposed to be, but she's somewhere in the library." Michelle hit a button, and a list of Sean's books printed out. She placed it on top of the stack. "But she knows we're supposed to leave at noon sharp."

"I didn't see her upstairs," Sean said. "I was studying in the stacks."

Michelle craned her neck to search the main room. "And she's not in here. She must still be down in the archives." She shrugged. "If she doesn't show up in a minute or so, I'll send her a text."

"Good idea," Sean said, collecting his books. "She probably lost track of time."

He thanked her and strode across the carpet to the library entrance, eager to get home and eat lunch before he went on shift. Taking the stairs two at a time, he descended to the main foyer, where one door led outside and another to storage rooms and archives.

There he hesitated, something telling him he shouldn't leave yet. Maybe he should locate Kara in the archives and find out how she was doing after last night's ordeal. He doubted she would want to talk to him. Then again, this was a chance to clarify that he did believe her about the intruder, despite the chief's questions.

The thought of his uncle made his stomach churn. All his life he'd looked up to his uncle and trusted him implicitly. But now the two of them appeared to be diverging in their viewpoints, something that was probably inevitable as Sean matured. There was a tug-of-war brewing in Sean's mind and heart—between the way things had always been and his own convictions.

With sudden resolve, Sean pivoted on his heel and reached for the door to the archives. The worst thing that could happen was that Kara would tell him to get lost. But at least she would know that he cared enough to follow up.

The overhead lights didn't come on when Sean stepped into the hallway, which was strange. He knew the lights in this hall had motion detectors. Tucking his books under his arm, he took out his phone and used the flashlight app to guide him.

There were no windows on this level, and the hallway with its closed doors seemed to press close. It was stuffy, the air full of the unmistakable scent of old paper.

The main archives were at the end, and if Kara was in there, she must be working in the dark. There wasn't a hint of light around the doorframe.

His footsteps slowed as he passed a couple of open doorways. "Kara?" he called. "Your mom's waiting for you."

The answer was a rush of air as someone charged out of one of the rooms.

Sean whirled around to see who it was, trying to aim his light on the person's face. "Stop! Police!" He wasn't on duty, but he felt no guilt about using his badge in this moment.

The figure kept running, heavy footsteps pounding on the tile. He—Sean was pretty sure the person was male—reached the door to the foyer and slammed through.

For a moment he was tempted to run after him, but that would probably be fruitless. Once outside the building, the person would be almost impossible to find.

Then a trickle of fear ran down his spine. Where was Kara? Had the man hurt her?

"Kara? Are you all right?" Sean sprinted to the archives room and burst through the door.

At first glance, the room appeared empty. He swung his light around, picking out bookshelves, filing cabinets, and workstations.

"Kara?" he called again. "It's Sean. Can you hear me?"

The answer was a whimper.

Heart in his throat, Sean walked around the room, searching for Kara. He found her at the very back, crouched in a gap between a filing cabinet and the wall.

In the light's beam, she peered up at him, her eyes filled with fear. "Is he gone?" she whispered.

"He is," he said, reaching for her hand. "He ran out of here as if his tail were on fire."

That ridiculous comment made Kara smile. She accepted his hand, her fingers so small in his, and stood, groaning as her limbs straightened.

Sean put an arm around her and led her to the closest chair, then guided her to sit. "What happened?" he asked, reluctantly releasing her. His arms felt strangely empty without her in them.

She sat huddled, her arms wrapped around her stomach. "I was down here working when I heard footsteps coming. Then the lights went out." She shuddered.

He clenched his fists. "Did he hurt you?"

"No. But I didn't exactly wait to find out. I used the light on my phone to find that hiding place and squeezed inside." Kara swallowed. "He came into the room, breathing heavily. It was the creepiest thing I've ever experienced."

"Then what?" Sean barked.

"He stood there for a few minutes, not saying a word. I didn't want to use my phone again because he might have seen the glow. And I couldn't call for help."

Sean could imagine the tension of those long, scary minutes all too well. Help and safety were within reach, but Kara had been trapped. He growled in anger.

She gave him a startled look.

"Sorry, but this is upsetting," he said. "You never expect something like this to happen in the college library during the day."

Kara studied his face in the glow of his flashlight app. "You're right. So was the person after me, or was it random?"

Sean didn't know which answer was worse. "I don't know, but I'm going to call security. If there's someone lurking around, the college needs to know."

"Let me gather my things, and we'll get out of here." She turned on her phone for additional light and moved to a workstation. "The lights still aren't working?"

Sean went to the switches at the door, where he could override the motion detector setting. He fiddled with the lever, but the lights didn't come on. "Nope. Another thing to report." He brought up the dial pad on his phone, ready to call security.

Kara gasped. "Look at this." She pointed at something on the desk.

Sean crossed the room in several long strides. A slip of paper lay on top of the work surface, a handwritten scrawl across it.

Quit digging around, or you'll be next.

Disbelief and fear shone in Kara's eyes. "That wasn't there before the lights went out. So the person must have left it for me."

Sean ached to give Kara a reassuring hug. Instead, he took a picture of the note, as was his duty. "What do you think it's referring to?"

"Probably Aunt Angela's death." She rubbed her hands up and down her arms, as if trying to get warm. "Maybe last night's intruder left it." Her voice was husky. "Which would mean they followed me here. But how did they know what I was doing?"

What *had* she been doing? Sean refrained from probing, although the microfilm machine revealed that she'd been reading newspaper articles. "I've got an evidence bag in my truck. I'll bag this up and take it to the station."

"Thank you for believing me," Kara said, a break in her voice. "I was worried—" She didn't need to finish the sentence. After the chief's attitude last night, anyone would be shy about talking to the police.

"I'm going to call security, and figure out what's wrong with these lights." He paced a few steps away to make the call. "Connect me to security, please."

Once he had someone, he gave a brief overview of the situation, including that the lights were out in the basement level.

Within a couple of minutes, heavy footsteps accompanied by muttered complaints and the jingle of a tool belt were heard. The door to the archives room opened, revealing a stocky man dressed in a maintenance worker's uniform. "What's going on with the lights?"

As Sean moved closer, he saw the name *Ernie* embroidered on his shirt pocket. "You tell us. Ms. Foxworth was working here when the lights went out on her. When I came downstairs later, I noticed they were out in the corridor too."

"I'd better check the breakers," Ernie said. "They shouldn't have tripped like that." He hitched up his trousers and turned to go.

"We'll wait here for security," Sean said.

"Suit yourself," Ernie muttered. He tromped off down the hall, calling a greeting to someone as he went.

This time a security guard arrived, a young man named Greg. "What can I do for you?" he asked. "Someone reported a stalker?"

"That was me," Sean said. He introduced himself and shook Greg's hand. "I happened to come down here when the person ran off. But let Ms. Foxworth tell you what happened."

The lights overhead came flickering on.

"And that's going to make things a whole lot easier," Sean commented.

Greg had a report form with him, and he took Kara through the questions, pausing when she said who her mother was. Of course he must know Michelle—everyone at the college did.

"So neither of you got a good look at this person, huh?" Greg asked. "It could have been a student or faculty member who came down to work but realized the lights weren't operating."

"Maybe you're right," Kara told the guard. "But why did he leave me that threatening note?" She pointed at the piece of paper.

"And why did he go tearing out of here?" Sean added.

Greg eyed the note, his blue eyes expressionless. "I don't have an answer for that. It must be a prank, and he didn't want to get caught."

Sean snorted. "I doubt it. But don't worry about it. I'm going to take the note into evidence. You might want a picture of it for your records, in case something like this happens again on campus."

Greg plucked at his lower lip with a finger. "You think so? I sure hope not. This is supposed to be the quiet time of year. Well, besides summer."

"Trouble never sleeps," Sean said, clapping the guard on the shoulder. "If I were you, I'd do a few extra patrols here in the library and around the campus in general."

Greg nodded.

Sean dug into his pocket and pulled out a card. "Send me a copy of your report, okay? We'll be a good example of that cross-jurisdictional cooperation Chief Colton and President Douglas are always talking about. Town and gown, right?"

The security guard grunted. He had Kara sign the report, then gave her one of the copies. "Call us if you have any more trouble."

"I'll do that," Kara said. She pulled the microfilm out of the machine and put it away, then grabbed her handbag and coat. "I'd better go meet Mom. She's going to wonder where I got to."

The two men had waited until Kara was ready to leave. Sean was reluctant to leave her alone down here. As for Greg, he probably felt the same way. Finally the trio made their way down the corridor.

At the exit door, Greg pushed ahead with a nod. "I'll be in touch later, Officer Colton. Take care, Ms. Foxworth."

"Hold on," Kara told Greg. "Please don't say anything to my mother, okay? I want to be the one to tell her about this."

"No problem," Greg said before walking through the door.

Kara turned to Sean. "I'm fine from here. Mom and I are going to lunch and then to an appointment. Oh, and to get fingerprinted at the station."

"Busy afternoon," Sean remarked. There was so much he wanted to tell her, but it all sounded pretty lame. Finally he said, "I'd like to give you my personal cell number. Please call me if anything else happens." He actually wanted to warn her to stay out of harm's way, but he had a sinking feeling it was too late. She'd been accosted twice in two days.

Kara took her phone out of her handbag, pressing the screen so she could enter his number. "All right, though I'll probably call 911 first."

Sean hesitated, not sure if he should say more. Then he went for it. "Absolutely. But I'm not just an officer. I'm a friend."

Her dark eyes were somber. "Are you?"

Any hope that coming to Kara's rescue had dissolved her reservations about him fled. He obviously had a long way to go before she trusted him fully again—if she ever did.

Kara rushed up the stairs to the first floor. At the top, she glanced down the stairwell. Sean was gone, the swing of the outside door the only sign he'd even been there.

Upstairs, her mother greeted her with a frown. "Where have you been? I was about ready to come find you."

"Sorry. I got caught up in the archives." Kara felt bad about the fib, but this wasn't the time or place to announce that she had been stalked by someone right in this building. Or that the person had left a threatening note. Too many people were around, and she was pretty sure no one else was in danger. She alone had been the target, not that she knew why. She hitched her bag higher. "Are you ready?"

Her mom's answer was to call to another librarian. "I'll be out the rest of the day. Personal time."

The librarian, a balding man wearing horn-rimmed glasses, smiled at them. "Have fun. See you tomorrow."

Outside, Kara was glad to find that the temperature had warmed slightly. Snow slid off the roof and softened along the shoveled walks. "I'm in the visitor lot," she said, leading the way.

They walked to Kara's car and were soon on their way downtown.

"It's so festive," Kara remarked as they drove along Main Street with its rows of charming storefronts. "They've really outdone themselves." She heard the false note in her cheerful tone and prayed her mother wouldn't pick up on it. There was so much to talk about that Kara dreaded beginning the conversation. It would be like opening the floodgates.

"Look. There's a parking space." Her mother pointed to a spot in front of their destination, Upper Crust Bakery & Café.

Kara slid into the space.

They exited the car and approached the door. Through the huge front window, Kara could see people seated at tables and lining up at the counter to order.

Cheery bells jingled as they entered the establishment redolent of fresh baked bread, coffee, and spices. In honor of the season, Christmas music played over the sound system, and colorful decorations adorned the space.

Kara smiled. "I love this place."

They dropped their coats at an empty table for two, then got in line. The wait gave Kara plenty of time to study the chalkboard menu with its array of choices. After much deliberation, she decided on a favorite—chipotle turkey with avocado, Swiss cheese, lettuce, tomato, and aioli on toasted country white. Her mom ordered a thick BLT on wheat toast. They also bought a bag of kettle chips to share and two large cups of iced tea.

Once at their table, Kara focused on eating her lunch. The delectable sandwich and the tangy salt-and-vinegar chips were worth her full attention. "Why do I like the folded chips so much?" she asked, pulling out one that reminded her of origami and popping it into her mouth.

"I have no idea," her mother said. "You've always been like that. You used to hunt through the bag and fish them all out."

A middle-aged woman at the counter grabbed a big sack of sandwiches and turned to go, her route leading her past their table. The woman stopped with a gasp. "Michelle, I was so sorry to hear about your sister-in-law."

Kara's mom set her sandwich down and wiped her fingers on a napkin. "Thank you. So was I." Her voice was level, betraying no emotion.

The woman turned to Kara. "This must be your daughter. Hello, dear, I'm Rhonda Peabody, the secretary at the police station."

"Nice to meet you," Kara said. Rhonda must know Sean, and maybe she knew even more about Angela's death than they did because of her position. "Did you know Aunt Angela well?"

Rhonda's heavily sprayed black hair didn't budge as she shook her head. "Only a little. But she was a wonderful woman. Everyone said so. It's a real loss."

"It is," her mother said. "We're still adjusting to the news."

"Oh, I'm sure." Rhonda stepped back. "I'm sorry to intrude. Please enjoy your lunch." She bustled toward the door.

Her mom watched Rhonda go, her eyes troubled. "*Now* they say she's wonderful." Her tone was bitter. "But I had to listen to gossip for years claiming that Angela ran away with someone. As if she would abandon all her responsibilities, family, and friends. And her almost-fiancé."

"Nelson," Kara said. At her mother's surprised look, she said, "I found a card from him next door this morning." Too late, she realized that she'd admitted going inside Angela's house. "It sounded like they were close."

Her mother leaned back in her chair with a sigh. "They were. I think he was about to propose."

"How sad." Kara's heart ached to think that the couple never had an opportunity to get married or raise a family. It was a real tragedy. Sensing that her mother was headed into a deep well of sorrow, Kara decided to change the subject. "You're going to kill me, but I did something kind of sneaky today."

Curiosity lit her mom's eyes. "You mean snooping around the house?" She had obviously noticed Kara's verbal slip a moment earlier.

"No, something probably worse." Kara hesitated. "I read the letter from Benedict Fuller. He wants to buy our house?"

Her mother's expression tightened. "He wants to buy the whole street in order to build upscale housing. The neighbors and I are fighting it."

"He can't make you sell, can he?" Kara asked, alarmed.

"Definitely not. Instead of each one of us dealing with him on our own, we've banded together. Otherwise, his strategy would be to chip away, property by property. A lot of our neighbors are elderly, so I'm sure he thinks they will be easy pickings. We're putting him on notice that they aren't."

"That's great." Kara felt a surge of admiration for her mother and the plucky neighbors. "Are you sure, though? You might get a lot of money for the houses."

The color had returned to her mother's cheeks. She picked up the sandwich and took a big bite, her appetite apparently restored. "I'm positive," she said after chewing and swallowing. "I love my home. And all those houses are historic. Once they're gone, they're gone. We can't let that happen."

"That's the spirit," Kara said. She checked her phone. "We'd better eat up. Our appointment is in twenty minutes."

Hill and Associates was located at the other end of Main Street in a gracious Queen Anne house repurposed as professional offices. Kara remembered coming by now and then with her mom to visit Angela at work. Sometimes the trio had gone from the office to lunch or on a quick shopping trip.

The place still looked the same—yellow with lots of lacy white trim and a tower. To Kara's young eyes, it had seemed a shame that the lovely house was used for mundane business purposes and not a personal residence.

After parking in a visitor spot, they made their way across the drive and through the portico to the double wooden doors.

Her mom hesitated with her hand on the brass door latch. "I really don't want to go in."

Kara understood. Once they went inside and heard the contents of Angela's will, she would truly be gone. She gave her mother a hug. "It's okay," she whispered. "We'll get through it somehow."

Her mom held her tight. "I know. I just had a weak moment, I guess."

"You're allowed." Kara reached around her and opened the door. "The sooner we go in, the sooner it will be over with."

They stepped into a spacious entrance hall with a curved staircase rising to the second floor. The plaster walls were painted a creamy white that contrasted with dark carved woodwork, and richly colored Persian area rugs provided spots of color.

A striking—and very pregnant—blonde woman was sitting behind the reception desk. With a thrill of shock, Kara recognized her. Tiffany Yates, her high school nemesis. The girl who had dated Sean behind Kara's back while they were still together.

Ah, the dramas of high school. At the time it had been a real tragedy, but she was over it, right? They were all adults now, and besides, judging by the hefty diamond Tiffany was wearing, she was married to someone else. If Tiffany recognized her, she didn't acknowledge it.

"Good afternoon," Tiffany said. "How can I help you?"

"Michelle and Kara Foxworth," her mother said. "We're here to see Walter."

"I'll let him know you're here." Tiffany picked up the telephone receiver and spoke into it. After a moment, she pointed to a door down the hall. "Go ahead. He's ready for you." She seemed to focus on her computer, but Kara sensed her watching them as they walked down the hall.

Kara glanced back at Tiffany. The other woman moved her head so fast her long hair swung. She *had* been staring at them.

Her mother knocked, then twisted the doorknob.

Walter Hill rose from behind his desk as they entered, a smile of greeting on his face. Walter was on the short side and slender, with a pointed nose and brown eyes. "Please sit down." His gesture was expansive as he indicated the visitor chairs placed in front of his desk.

Once they were seated, he sat again, clasping his hands on top of the desk. His face sobered. "It's sad business that brings us here together today. I'm so sorry for your loss." He cleared his throat. "And ours. Angela was an exemplary employee."

"Thank you." Her mother pulled a tissue out of her purse and held it tightly in her fist. "At least we know the truth and can begin the healing process."

The truth? Kara understood why her mother put it that way, but she wasn't convinced that they knew the whole story yet. All they knew was that Angela had suffered a car accident.

"Yes, it definitely is a process." Walter picked up papers and tapped the sides to straighten them. "I have Angela's will here, which I think you've seen in the past, Michelle, since she gave you permission to manage her financial affairs."

"She had permission to manage mine," her mom added. "We set it up that way after Miles died. In case something happened to one of us, the other could continue to take care of Kara and the houses."

"Very wise," Walter said. Standing, he pushed the papers across the desk. "Please read it over and let me know if you have any questions."

Kara scooted her chair closer so she could read each page after her mother was done. Everything was pretty basic, with her mom inheriting everything. If she had predeceased Angela, Kara was next in line.

There was one notable exception. An embroidered picture of a covered bridge worked by Angela was to go to Nelson Reed.

Kara stifled a gasp. What an odd legacy. Yes, it was beautiful, but had he really liked it that much? She realized the other two were staring at her. "Sorry. I was surprised about her leaving the covered bridge art to Nelson."

"It must have been a sentimental favorite," Walter said. "Although I expected her to change that provision, the way things were going."

"What do you mean?" Kara asked. Was he implying that Angela had a reason to change her will? Did he believe the story that Angela had left town with another man? As her employer, he might know if she had been seeing someone else.

Walter waved his hand. "My apologies. I spoke out of turn. It's all water under the bridge, like in that picture of Angela's." He chuckled. "Do you have any questions?"

"No, this is pretty straightforward," her mother answered. "I assume it all has to go through probate to be finalized."

"That's correct," Walter said. "It shouldn't take long since Angela had a will. So many people don't. And there were no debts or claims against her estate that you are aware of?"

"Not even a mortgage," her mom said. "Angela lived a very frugal lifestyle."

A speculative gleam lit his brown eyes. "I understand your neighborhood is slated for a building project."

Her mother laughed shortly. "Only if we sell. It's not a done deal yet."

Walter sat down. "As we've discussed in the past, wise property management and decisions are an important piece of personal financial planning. Now that you officially own your sister-in-law's home, you've got a sizable asset there."

"I'm not ready to even think about that," her mother said, her tone brisk enough to close the subject. "If there's nothing else, we have another appointment."

Walter stood. "We're all set for now. I'll keep you posted as things move through the channels." He came around the desk to escort them to the door, where he shook their hands. "Nice seeing you both. Take care, and I'll be in touch."

Kara slipped out into the hall, feeling as if she were escaping something. She'd always liked Walter, who had been something of an unofficial uncle, given his working relationship with her aunt, but now she wasn't sure if he had her mother's best interests at heart. Which would certainly disqualify him as her attorney. And that comment about the covered bridge artwork. The more she thought about it, the more she was convinced he'd been referring to the rumors about Angela having a secret relationship.

"I'm going to the restroom for a minute," her mother said. "Be right back."

The restroom was down the hall, so Kara lingered in the entrance hall. She was racking her brain for something to say to Tiffany when the front door opened.

A tall young man with broad shoulders swept into the building, pulling a wool cap off his blond head. He wore a leather jacket, trim dark jeans, and boots.

Neil Fuller, Benedict Fuller's son. Kara had gone to high school with Neil. He'd been a year ahead, captain of the soccer team, hotshot skier, and all around big man on campus.

Too big to notice her existence, that was for sure. So why was he smiling at her now as if she were the best thing he'd seen in days?

"Hey," he said as he drew closer to her. "I didn't know you were back in town."

"I'm here for the holidays," Kara said. "How are you?"

Neil rocked back on his heels, beaming. "I'm great. For the past couple of years, I've been running Fuller Construction—you know, the building arm of Fuller Property Partners."

"I've heard of it," Kara said. She also wondered if Neil was behind the proposed purchase of the houses on her street. Did he think of their demolition as an opportunity for a career-building project?

Neil stuck his hands into his pockets, his smile confident and bright. "We should get together later and catch up. Maybe have dinner."

"I don't know," Kara began, her immediate instinct being to refuse. But then she thought, *Why not?* He obviously still liked to talk about himself, so maybe she could learn more about the inner workings of the Benedict empire and glean something that would help her mother and their neighbors.

She pasted a wide and very fake smile on her face. "On second thought, that sounds great." She pulled out her phone. "Why don't you give me your number? I'll see how the rest of today shapes up." That way she could call him at her leisure.

Neil recited his number to her, then strolled over to the reception desk, whistling. "Is he ready for me?"

"Go ahead," Tiffany said.

After Neil disappeared through Walter's door, Kara said to Tiffany, "How have you been? I see congratulations are in order."

Tiffany beamed, placing both hands on her abdomen. "Thank you. I'm happy." She moved a photo on her desk so Kara could see it. "*We're* happy. That's my husband, Jake. He's the manager at the ski area."

"That's wonderful," Kara said. And she meant it. Any lingering animosity toward the other woman really was gone.

"How are you?" Tiffany's pretty blue eyes shone with sympathy. "I was so sorry to hear about your aunt. I'm still trying to fill her shoes, even though I've been here several years now."

"We're okay," Kara said. "I'm glad I could be with Mom when we found out."

Tiffany nodded. "That must be a comfort." Then, glancing over her shoulder as if making sure no one was within earshot, she whispered, "Be careful, okay?"

Before Kara could press her for an explanation, the restroom door opened and her mother emerged.

Tiffany bent her head to her keyboard and began to pound away, making it clear that she was finished talking. Was she warning her about Neil? He had been another of Tiffany's high school boyfriends. In fact, they'd dated quite a long time.

Or was she referring to something else entirely?

A fter a quick sandwich at home, Sean put on his uniform and duty belt, planning to go to the station early. He wouldn't clock in for the extra time, but he wanted to make a report about Kara's stalker and log the note. This incident, combined with the break-in at Angela Foxworth's house, told Sean something: the discovery of Angela's body had set things in motion. Bad things. And Kara was in the crosshairs.

"We're going to take care of her, aren't we?" he asked Bandit, who was watching him get ready.

Bandit mewed, and Sean took that as agreement. Bandit was a very intelligent cat.

When Sean arrived at the station, he was surprised to see Ryan sitting at the desk.

Ryan glanced at him. "You aren't due in until three."

"I know," Sean said, unzipping his jacket. "Where's Rhonda?"

Ryan swiveled in Rhonda's chair. "She went out to pick up sandwiches. The crash reconstruction team is due here at one." This team was a function of the Vermont State Police, and it was called in for serious accidents.

Sean froze. He hadn't been informed of the meeting. This was either an oversight or a deliberate omission, since he normally sat in on these sessions. He hated to think the latter. "Good thing I'm early then."

"Good thing," Ryan muttered.

Sean hung up his coat and proceeded to his desk, located in a corner of the squad room. In addition to the chief and Rhonda, there were half a dozen officers. Dispatch was handled jointly with several other towns, allowing them to have round-the-clock coverage. The other officers on duty were out on patrol, and the other night officer wasn't in yet.

When Sean logged on to his computer, a flag came up saying he had a new e-mail. Greg had e-mailed Kara's report about the incident at the college as well as one of his own. He had searched the library basement and patrolled the grounds, looking for anyone he deemed suspicious.

Good man. Sean was sure the prowler was long gone, but he appreciated Greg taking the incident seriously. He sent back a note to that effect before starting his own report.

The door to the station opened, and Rhonda bustled in, carrying a paper sack. She stopped short when she saw Sean. "How late am I?" she joked.

"I'm early," he assured her with a grin.

She took off her coat and hung it up. "I've got lunch if you're here for the meeting."

"I am, but I already ate, thanks." Sean continued typing.

Ryan was propping open the door to the conference room, a sign that the meeting was about to begin.

Rhonda picked up the bag and headed that way, then stopped by his desk. "I saw Michelle and Kara Foxworth when I was picking these up." She made a sympathetic noise. "Poor things. I feel so bad for them."

"Me too," Sean said. He sent his report to the printer. "Need any help getting ready?"

"No, I'm all set," Rhonda said. "I'm going to make a pot of coffee and put out some water and soft drinks. Thanks for offering." She continued on her way.

Sean read over the report one more time. Now that he had a case number, he needed to log the note into the evidence system and put it in the locker. Who could have done such a thing? And why? What was it the stalker was afraid Kara would find?

A solid hand landed on his shoulder, making him jump. "What are you working on?" Chief Colton asked.

Sean turned to face him. "This morning while I was studying at the college library, someone stalked Kara Foxworth and left her a threatening note." He held up the evidence bag. "She was working down in the basement when the perp switched off the lights and scared her."

The chief stared at the note, his expression inscrutable. "Probably a prank. You know how those college kids are."

"The kids who are now on holiday break?" Sean couldn't resist pointing out. "Regardless, she was unsettled by the incident and filed a report with campus security. Since I was there, I decided to log it as a stalking incident in our records. You never know—the person might try something like this again off campus." He mentioned that to forestall the chief saying that it was purely under campus jurisdiction since it had occurred there. "Besides, it may be related to the break-in at Angela Foxworth's house."

"There's a stretch if I ever heard one," the chief said. "But that's not what I came to talk to you about. The accident reconstruction team is convening shortly, and I want you to sit in on the meeting."

This invitation helped soothe Sean's doubts and hurt feelings about being left out. It must have been an oversight that he didn't get notice of the meeting. "Sure. I'm about done here, so I'll be right with you."

The station door opened, and two state troopers entered.

"There they are," the chief said, striding off to welcome them.

Sean quickly made up two file folders for copies of the report, one for Rhonda and one for him. He always kept copies of his open cases handy.

"Thank you for joining us today," Chief Colton said once everyone was seated around the table. He introduced Sergeant Rebecca Lee and Trooper Todd Stevens. In addition to Sean, Ryan was the only other Castlebridge officer present. "We're a small team here. That's why we're grateful to have your expertise."

Sergeant Lee nodded. "We're glad to be of help. As you know, the state police in Vermont have jurisdiction over major crimes because towns and police forces are so small. But in reverse, we can't do our jobs without you."

Very gracefully put, Sean thought. She'd managed to assert authority while allowing the chief to keep his dignity. As always when he was around state troopers, Sean absorbed every detail of how they operated. He figured the more he knew, the better he would do once he was on board.

"Before we get started, please help yourselves to some food." The chief gestured to the lunch set out on the credenza.

"Don't mind if I do," Trooper Stevens said, standing up.

"This one is always hungry," Sergeant Lee said, also rising.

Trooper Stevens patted his trim stomach as he stood back to let his superior go first. "What can I say? I'm a growing boy."

Sean and the others held back to let the guests go first, although Ryan practically fell over himself to assist the attractive sergeant. Suppressing an eye roll, Sean waited until last to grab a soft drink.

They ate for a few minutes, chatting about traffic, the weather, and ski conditions at the local mountains.

Then Sergeant Lee got down to business. She and her team had used an array of technology to reconstruct the accident. While Trooper

Stevens ran the laptop, the sergeant took them through the event from start to finish.

One heartbreaking point related to where Angela had gone off the road. That particular spot was marked by a steep drop-off—and a lack of mature trees until right before the ravine, where she had hit a big pine.

Sergeant Lee used her pointer to indicate what she meant. "This explains why the vehicle traveled so far down the bank. If the rail had been there or she'd crashed either before or after that spot, she still might have died, but the accident would have been readily visible."

The chief put down his sandwich, his complexion pale. "The rail went up the next summer. This confirms what a dangerous spot it was."

Sean thought back to the retrieval of Angela's car. The tow truck had backed up so that the bed was extended over the rail. The driver had winched the car up the bank and onto the flatbed. Sean had been so rattled then that he hadn't put it together, but he could learn from this. He would work on sharpening his observational skills.

Sean couldn't help but wonder why she had crashed right there. It wasn't at the apex of the curve, the spot where other accidents had occurred.

"Do you think road conditions were a factor?" Sean asked.

Both the chief and Ryan looked at him, and he wondered if he'd spoken out of turn.

"Good question," Sergeant Lee said. "We pulled road condition reports for the night Ms. Foxworth was last seen. In this area there was bare roadway and no new precipitation. But there might have been localized ice. In a couple of spots, drainage isn't that good, so some areas do tend to ice over."

Sean had noticed that himself, and he knew where to be cautious. Wouldn't that have been true of Angela too? She'd lived in Castlebridge all her life.

He realized he was trying to make a case for foul play. Why? Because he had an uneasy feeling, an intuition that something wasn't right.

After concluding the discussion about the accident itself, Sergeant Lee moved on to observations about Angela's injuries, using a copy of the autopsy and information about the car's condition. She explained that Angela had most likely died of a head injury suffered when the vehicle came to rest. Cracks in the windshield bore out this theory.

And then she revealed what Sean deeply sensed was a smoking gun.

"To verify the observation made by the medical examiner," Sergeant Lee said, "these cracks are consistent with the victim not wearing a seat belt."

Sean glanced at his fellow officers, trying to gauge if they grasped the import of this statement. Both were impassive, listening without comment or reaction.

What did Angela's missing seat belt mean? That she'd gotten careless? She didn't drink, and there was no evidence of prescription medicine. Maybe he should ask Michelle if Angela had been ill. If all these inquiries led nowhere, there was only one option left.

Someone had made sure that Angela was unbelted when her vehicle traveled down that slope.

It took a minute, but Sean forced his attention back to the presentation. He needed to set his speculations aside and, like a true detective, examine all the facts without bias. And stop thinking about Kara. That was a recipe for clouded judgment. The best thing he could do for her and her mother was discover the truth.

Then they could truly put Angela to rest.

After the troopers left, with Sean making sure to get their cards, he did some paperwork at his desk. Movement on the Foxworth break-in was halted until Kara and Michelle provided prints for elimination. He made a note to call them if they didn't come in today. He smiled to himself. There went his resolve not to think about Kara.

He needed to run some other matters by the chief, so he gathered his files and knocked on his uncle's office door. "Is this a good time?"

Chief Colton replaced his phone receiver with a sigh. "Good as any. Come on in."

As they went through the paperwork, Sean noticed that his uncle seemed unwell. His complexion was pasty, and he kept mopping his forehead with a handkerchief. "Are you all right? Are you coming down with something?"

The chief tucked away his handkerchief. "It's not me. It's Peggy."

Sean's stomach lurched. Aunt Peggy had suffered from breast cancer last year. "It's not—" He couldn't bring himself to even say the word.

The chief shook his head. "Thankfully her checkups have been fine. But her rheumatoid arthritis is acting up. She's pretty miserable."

"I'm sorry to hear that," Sean said. He knew the condition was chronic and painful. "Is there anything you can do?" New treatments and medications were being developed all the time, maybe for this illness too.

The chief gave a short laugh. "Move to Florida near our son and your parents. Living in a warm, sunny climate would help her immensely."

Sean wanted to ask why his aunt and uncle didn't make plans to go, but he sensed the question wouldn't be welcome. He wasn't privy to the chief's financial situation or other factors that might hinder their relocation. So he kept quiet, allowing the chief to say as much or as little as he wanted.

His uncle sighed. "I suppose I could put in for early retirement, maybe pick up another position down there. But I'm not quite there financially, so it's a risk. I hate to uproot Peggy if we're not going to be on solid footing. She doesn't need the stress."

"I hear you," Sean said softly.

Chief Colton leaned back in his chair and rocked, making it squeak. "If I do go, there could be a good opportunity for you here."

Sean gaped at him. "You mean a promotion to chief?" He'd never really thought about it because being a small-town chief with all the politics didn't appeal to him. Chief Colton didn't spend much time actually solving crimes. His role was more administrative. He had to focus on the budget, staffing, equipment, and educational and legal requirements.

The chief tapped on the desk with his palm. "Exactly what I'm saying. You've got the brains and the heart. Unfortunately this role comes with a whole lot of baggage."

"You mean dealing with the select board?" Sean guessed. This board of three local residents had the power to hire—and fire—the chief of police. They could smooth the path for a chief or make the position a nightmare.

"That's right," Chief Colton said. "I've had good boards and others not so good. Some people don't have a notion as to what is required for a solid force and will nickel and dime you to death over the most insignificant things." An undertone of disgust had crept into his tone. "Sure, I have a so-called good job, but there isn't enough money in the world to make up for the aggravation some days."

Sean chuckled. "You're making a really convincing argument for me to apply when the time comes."

The chief laughed. "I suppose I am. But if you want to stay in law enforcement in Vermont, your options are limited. There isn't much upward mobility." He thumbed his chest. "This is as high as you can go, unless you join the troopers like you're hoping."

"That's what I'm aiming for," Sean said. Castlebridge was fortunate in that they had very little serious crime. That being said, his dream job of detective with the state police meant being immersed in serious crimes, but at least he would be actively investigating, putting perpetrators away, and obtaining justice for victims. These were very concrete and vital goals. He would be making a difference.

The chief rocked in his chair again. "Anyway, if you don't have anything else for me, I'll let you get back to work."

Sean checked the clock. "Yeah, I've got to get ready to go out on patrol." He rose from the uncomfortable seat and stretched. "Tell Aunt Peggy I'm thinking about her."

"Will do," Chief Colton said, shuffling papers on his desk. "I'm sure she'll want you to come over for a meal later this week."

"Sounds good." Sean picked up his files and slipped out of the office.

His steps stuttered when he entered the main room. Kara and Michelle were standing at the reception desk. So they'd made it in after all. Sean headed in that direction.

"The Foxworths are here to have fingerprints taken," Rhonda told Sean. "Ryan offered to do it since you're going out on patrol." Her expression was apologetic, since she knew it was his case.

"That's fine," Sean said, annoyed but not wanting to make a big deal about it. Ryan was always at his heels. "Thanks for coming in," he said to Kara and her mother. "I was just thinking that having your prints on file will help us move forward on the case."

"Why are we doing this again?" Michelle asked, a worried look on her face. "I've never had my fingerprints taken."

"For the process of elimination," Sean assured her. "No other reason. When we investigated the break-in at your sister-in-law's house, we found a lot of fingerprints. Yours will help us narrow them down to sets we should investigate further."

"Glad we can help," Kara said, regarding him from under lowered lashes.

Sean couldn't read her expression, and everything about her body language—her stiff shoulders, her folded arms—warned him to keep his distance. He gritted his teeth. *Message received.*

But he was still going to do his best to figure out who was terrorizing Kara. And why and how Angela Foxworth had ended up dead.

"What shall we do now?" her mother asked Kara as they left the police station.

Although Kara was weighed down with all the events and revelations of the past day—had it really been less than twenty-four hours?—she decided a break would help them both. "Why don't we get a Christmas tree?" Visiting a farm to cut their own tree had been one of their favorite holiday rituals. Since her father's death, they hadn't been once.

"Really?" her mom asked. "You want to?"

"I do," Kara said. "Why don't we swing by and pick up your car and then change at home?" Their outfits were too dressy for trudging through snow.

A short while later, they were once again in Kara's car and driving out toward Everly's Evergreens, their favorite tree farm. The route took them past Nelson's dairy farm, and since there wasn't any traffic behind them, Kara slowed as they went by.

It was a beautiful property, classic Vermont. A white farmhouse, big red barn, and grazing pastures were set in a natural bowl rimmed by rolling hills. Rows of sugar maples lined the long driveway, reminding Kara of the syrup she had enjoyed that morning.

"I can't believe Angela left Nelson that picture," Kara mused. "What a strange gift."

"I agree. Perhaps it had some special meaning between the two of them." Her mother sighed. "I haven't seen Nelson in years. I feel a bit guilty about that. But back then I wondered if he had something to do with her leaving."

Surprise jolted Kara. "You mean that he might have done something to her?" she squeaked.

"Of course not. I thought maybe they'd had a fight and she took off. That sounds so lame when I say it out loud. Angela wasn't the type to take off in a hissy fit."

Kara pressed the gas pedal again. "Well, you were trying to make sense out of a very unusual situation. If only . . ." She left the sentence unfinished. *If only* Angela had crashed within view of the road. *If only* she hadn't had the accident at all. She stopped the direction of her thoughts. She'd already been down this road when her father died.

"I want to go see Nelson," Kara said. "Maybe tomorrow. I'll ask him about the covered bridge embroidery. If that's okay with you."

"I don't mind," her mother said. "It's past time to do something. I have to work, so you can tell him we're both thinking of him. And that a dinner invitation will be forthcoming." She made a little sound of disgust. "I owe him one after ignoring him for ten years."

"Don't beat yourself up too badly," Kara said. "He hasn't come to see you either, has he?"

"That's true. We've been in mutual avoidance mode, I guess." Her mom sat straighter in her seat. "But the time for that is over."

"I'll pass along the message," Kara said. "How much farther to the tree farm? I've forgotten."

Her mother gazed at the passing countryside. "A few more miles. Once we cross the brook, we're almost there."

The road was winding and hilly. As Kara descended one of the short but steep hills, she saw a large pickup approaching fast behind them. The truck was painted a dull black and sported oversize tires.

The bumper was dented and rusted, and the fenders and front license plate were covered in mud.

"Slow down," Kara muttered, glancing in the rearview mirror. Ahead was a steep, banked curve so she didn't want to speed up.

The throaty roar of the truck grew louder.

Her mom twisted in her seat and made a face. "Some people don't know how to drive."

Gripping the wheel so tightly her knuckles hurt, Kara took the curve. Her father had taught her how to drive, and she could hear his voice in her head. *Halfway through the curve, accelerate. Allow the vehicle's momentum to work for you, not against you.*

Grateful that she had good tires and her little sedan handled well, Kara sailed around the curve.

The truck remained close on her bumper, moving forward, then backing off slightly, as though eager to pass.

This was a terrible place for that, and Kara hoped the truck wouldn't try it. Traffic from the other direction wasn't visible, and such a move might cause a horrible accident.

Once out of the curve, the road straightened. He could pass. She slowed, hoping he would take the hint, and when he didn't, she unrolled her window and gestured with her hand.

The truck remained right behind her, a few scant feet from her bumper.

Her mother turned around again. "I don't like this. Is the driver trying to scare us? Why not go around us?"

"I don't know." Kara heard the terse note in her voice. "Sorry. I guess he's freaking me out." She slowed again, hoping he would leave. No such luck.

Another curve loomed. Kara sped up, trusting that her car and her driving skills would take them around it safely.

They made it through that one, and once again, the truck closed the distance between them.

"Don't pull over," her mom said, a note of panic in her voice. "The driver probably wants you to." She fumbled for her phone in her handbag. "I'm calling the police."

"I'm not pulling over," Kara said. "No way." She'd heard of situations where men had forced women motorists off the road. Many of those women had died. *Is that what happened to Angela?*

Her mother tossed her phone back into her bag. "I don't have a signal. Figures."

"Oh no!" Kara cried as the bridge over the Castle River came into view. She tensed even more when she realized that one lane was closed due to construction. Crossing the narrow bridge put them in a very vulnerable position. A set of ancient guardrails would be all that stood between them and the freezing river below.

To her dismay, she saw an old Volvo station wagon puttering along from the other direction. Since there wasn't a traffic light guarding the bridge, whoever got there first would cross first. Traffic from each direction alternated. All Vermonters understood this etiquette, instilled by generations of travel across one-lane covered bridges.

Kara quickly calculated time, distance, and speed in her mind. Could she do it? Should she? *Yes.* "Hold on," she told her mom.

Bracing her body, she pressed the gas pedal and surged forward, bearing down on the bridge.

The Volvo continued to approach. It would be close, but she would beat the other vehicle. She hoped.

Kara raced across the bridge, eyes on the road, ignoring the barrier on one side and the frail guardrail on the other. She was an arrow, shot straight and true.

Three things happened at once. She reached the other side, tires firmly gripping the road. The Volvo swerved into her lane to cross over behind her. And the big truck braked sharply to avoid a head-on collision with the tanklike Volvo.

A moment later, the truck driver did a three-point turn and roared off back the way he had come, driving a decent distance behind the other vehicle.

He hadn't just been an aggressive driver. He'd been following them on purpose. Cold sweat flashed over Kara's body at the realization of their near miss.

Her first impulse was to call Sean. Then she hesitated. He seemed to have an odd knack for showing up whenever things happened to her. Because he was involved?

No way. The strength of this instinctive reaction told her something. She *wanted* to trust Sean. Even crazier than that, she wanted their old friendship back. The easy give-and-take, the laughter, the way he understood her—

Her mother put a hand on her arm, interrupting her thoughts. "How did you learn to drive like that?"

Kara seized on the change of topic. "Dad. He made sure I knew how to handle a car under all kinds of conditions. And to trust my instincts."

"I should have known." Her mom shook her head. "Especially since he used to be an amateur rally racer. He could have gone pro."

"He was good enough." Kara had always enjoyed hearing stories about this chapter of her father's history. "But don't worry. I have no plans to take up the sport."

Her mother picked up her phone. "*Now* I have a signal. Should I call the police and report that driver?"

Kara thought for a moment. "I don't think it will do any good.

I couldn't read the license plate, so all we know is that he was driving a big black truck."

"He? You could see the driver?"

"No," Kara admitted. "The windshield had a glare. I guess I was assuming it was a man." The truck seemed like something a man would drive, plus she hadn't seen many women drive that aggressively.

"Well, I'm certainly going to keep my eyes peeled for that thing," her mom said tartly as she dropped her phone into her handbag. "If I get a chance, I'm going to give that driver a piece of my mind."

"Please don't. He might be dangerous or crazy. Or both."

A sign came into view, announcing that they were a mile from the tree farm.

"Thank goodness," Kara said. "We're almost there."

A few other vehicles were in the small lot. Families were choosing a tree in the open shed or wandering through a snowy field filled with beautifully shaped evergreens.

As Kara pulled into a spot, her heart rate slowed to normal. She resolved to forget their near miss and enjoy the occasion. After making sure she had mittens and her hat, she climbed out of the car. "All set?"

Her mother tugged a wool cap over her ears. "Sure am. Let's grab a hacksaw."

A bucket of saws free to borrow sat near the door to the shed, and they walked over.

"Cutting your own?" a teenage boy asked. "Good deal." He showed them a coded poster holding tags. "These tell you the kind of tree. The price varies by height."

"We've been here many times," Kara assured him. She'd also been here with Sean when they were in high school. "I love the balsam firs the best. They smell so good." Sean had thought so too. After chasing her down a long row, he'd kissed her next to the perfect tree, then cut it down for her. Her heart warmed at the sweet memory.

"Don't they?" The young man smiled. "Have fun. I'll see you when you're ready to check out."

Her mom took a saw, and the two women tramped across the parking lot and into the field. There they went up and down the rows, examining each tree critically.

"We have to be careful it isn't too big," her mother said. "They look smaller out here."

"I've made that mistake before," Kara said with a laugh. Like the tree Sean had cut. They'd had to shorten the trunk once they got it back to her house so it wouldn't hit the ceiling.

As Kara watched her mother study every tree, she felt a rush of love and hope. She was so grateful for this moment, one of the small yet precious events that make up a life. After losing her father and aunt, she'd learned not to take anything for granted.

That evening Kara got ready for her date with Neil. After learning they had reservations at Castlebridge's best restaurant, she borrowed a dress and pumps from her mother. She'd only brought casual clothing with her, with the exception of dress pants and a cashmere sweater for church. But that outfit wouldn't do for a formal dinner.

Thankful they were the same size—and her mom's taste was classic—Kara felt perfectly appropriate in the flowing black velvet dress. She actually enjoyed getting dressed up in anticipation of a nice meal out.

Neil arrived on time, handsome in jacket and slacks, no tie. He spent a few minutes chatting with Kara's mom, complimenting her on the house and asking about her work at the library.

After they said goodbye, Neil gallantly escorted Kara to his red Audi and held the door for her. During the short drive to the restaurant, they made pleasant small talk.

When they arrived at the restaurant, Neil hurried around the car and opened the door for her, then ushered her inside.

"Let me," Neil said, reaching to take her coat. He hung it up for her in the cloakroom, then placed his beside it.

The young, pretty hostess greeted them with a toothy smile. "Two for dinner?"

Neil squared his shoulders. "Reservation for Fuller."

The hostess scanned the list, pausing. "Not the party of six?"

"Six?" Neil frowned. "Oh, that's right. Dad is here tonight." He leaned closer to the hostess and whispered confidentially, "But we prefer to dine alone."

"Got it," the hostess said, picking up two menus. "Follow me."

As she led them through the restaurant, Kara heard a bray of laughter and searched the room for its source. Neil was right. His father, Benedict—tall and distinguished, resembling an older Neil—was seated with Everett Douglas and Walter Hill. The men's attractive wives rounded out the party.

"We'll go over in a minute," Neil told Kara. "I know they'll want to say hello."

Must we? But she couldn't think of a polite way to refuse. Walter, the family attorney, was all right, but she could do without talking to the other men. Everett had been insufferable at the library, and Benedict was trying to pressure her mother to sell their home.

Kara steeled herself for the encounter. These men might hold answers to what was going on with Angela's accident, the stalkers at the college and on the road, and the break-in at Angela's. If she had to choose three citizens with their fingers firmly on the pulse of the town, it would be Walter, Everett, and Benedict.

The hostess placed the menus on a table for two adorned with white linen, flowers, and a flickering candle. "Here you are. Your server will be right with you."

Neil helped Kara into her seat. "We'll go over after we order, okay? I don't know about you, but I'm starving."

Kara was hungry, but the anxiety she now felt about the date was quickly stealing her appetite. Not that she would admit it. "I've heard the food here is great," she said, opening the menu. "What do you recommend?"

Neil preened at the request, taking her through the various areas of the menu and making suggestions.

In the end, they decided on a warm brie appetizer, trout for Kara, and prime rib for Neil. The server took their order and delivered the ice water both requested.

"Let's go," Neil said, standing. He waited for Kara, then led her across the restaurant to his parents' table.

Kara couldn't help but feel the stares as they passed other diners. Neil was not only well-known but also strikingly handsome and self-assured. Kara did her best to keep her chin up and her shoulders straight, feigning a confidence she didn't exactly feel. This was not her preferred social scene at all.

The three couples looked up as they approached, the women scrutinizing Kara.

At least that was how it felt to her. Kara cranked up the wattage of her smile a few notches, resolved not to let them intimidate her.

"Hey, everyone," Neil said. "How are you all doing tonight?"

The older adults answered with assurances that they were well.

Neil put an arm around Kara's shoulders. "I'd like you to meet an old friend of mine. We went to high school together, and I was lucky enough to run into her earlier." He nodded to Walter. "At your office, sir."

"Even an old man like me remembers," Walter said with a laugh. "It was earlier today, after all. Wasn't it?"

The others joined in with chuckles.

Neil proceeded to introduce Kara, going around the table in order. Everett said that he knew her well since her mother worked at the college. As for Benedict, he eyed Kara appraisingly, saying nothing of the deal he was trying to strike with her mother.

After a few uncomfortable moments, Neil finally relented. "We'll let you get back to your meal," he said, guiding Kara away.

Back at their table, he again pulled out Kara's chair.

Although she didn't object, she wished he would quit the kid-glove treatment. She appreciated chivalry, but Neil was almost over the top.

"Perfect timing," the server said, setting their appetizer in the middle of the table. "Enjoy." She buzzed away.

Kara loved warm brie, but tonight it tasted like chalk. She didn't belong in this restaurant or with Neil. She felt like a fake. To be honest, her style was Upper Crust or even the local diner. She and Sean had often gone to the diner after the movies or a game to have ice cream or pie. While eating the sweet treats, they would laugh and simply enjoy being together.

"So," Neil said with soulful eyes as he scooped cheese onto a cracker, "tell me about yourself."

Tell him what? About her job? Her hobbies? The fact that she was incredibly out of place here? "What do you want to know?" she finally countered, laughing. "It's such a broad question."

He popped the cracker into his mouth and chewed. "Start with what you did after high school graduation. You got out ten years ago, right? A year after me."

"Yes," Kara said. "I went to the University of Vermont. Got a degree in library science, then my master's. I'm a school librarian in Massachusetts."

"Like mother, like daughter," Neil said, preparing another cracker. "Chip off the old block."

"I guess I could say the same about you," Kara replied before he could deliver another cliché. "Following in your dad's footsteps."

"Yes, that's true." Neil shrugged. "But what else was I going to do? He's done very well for himself. It didn't make sense for me to go somewhere else and work for another company. My degree from Clemson is in construction management."

Kara had to agree that Neil's path was the obvious one. But was he also carrying on his father's less-than-stellar ethical practices? Although nothing had yet risen to the level of a crime—as far as she knew—Benedict was known as a sharp businessman unafraid to apply pressure to both government officials and local residents. And he was currently applying that pressure to her mother and the other residents of their neighborhood.

Glad to take the focus off her life, Kara said, "Tell me about your projects. They must be so interesting." She honestly didn't care, but she thought he would enjoy it. Men with large egos loved to talk about themselves. Besides, she wanted to know if he was working on plans for her mom's neighborhood.

Before he could reply, the server arrived at their table, two large plates in hand. She placed their meals, then collected the remains of the appetizer. "Can I get you anything else?" She glanced at the level of their glasses. "Besides more water?"

"More water would be great," Kara said. "Thank you."

For a couple of minutes, they sampled their food. The trout was flaky and perfectly seasoned, and the mashed potatoes were divine, full of cream and butter. The steamed asparagus accompanying them was crisp but tender, lightly bathed in a lemon vinaigrette.

"What do you think?" Neil asked, cutting into his slab of prime rib. "Good, huh?"

"Yes," Kara agreed. "Delicious."

Across the room, the party of six was standing up, getting ready to leave.

Kara intercepted a speculative expression from Benedict, and she nodded in response. She contemplated what he thought of his son dating the daughter of a librarian. Surely he hoped for more of an equal partner in wealth and status for his son. Not that there were any worries here. After this dinner, Kara didn't plan to go out with Neil again. Despite his looks, charm, and wealth, he was not her type.

She wondered if Sean was still her type. As an image of his handsome face, endearing smile, and kind eyes floated into her mind, she had to admit that he was. But so what? He lived here. She lived in Massachusetts.

And she was far from ready to dive into anything beyond friendship, not to mention the fact that they had some old baggage to put to rest before they could even—

"Is everything all right?" Neil asked. "You seem lost in thought over there."

"Sorry. I was focusing on my food." Kara forked up another mouthful of potatoes. "It's so good."

"Yeah, this is my favorite place," Neil said. "For business and pleasure." He didn't say which category she was in.

"So, about your job," Kara said brightly. "What's your most interesting venture right now?"

His eyes lit up. "Dad has finally put me in charge of a really big project from concept to construction. We're calling it Castlebridge Village."

"That's a charming name," Kara said. "Residential development?"

"Mostly. Some commercial for the people who live there. It'll be right in the heart of downtown near Main Street and the college." He named the streets bordering the area.

Kara's stomach clenched. He was talking about her mother's neighborhood. "Great location."

Neil leaned forward, his expression eager. "It's the next logical area of town to undergo revitalization." He stabbed a finger onto the tablecloth while making his points. "Old but not historic. In need of upgraded infrastructure like roads and water systems. And we need more housing. This project will double population density in that area while maintaining green space. We're even putting in walking paths to connect everything."

All of that sounded good—until you considered that real people with homes were going to be impacted. "Won't this price out the people who already live there?"

"It might," he admitted. "But they'll get plenty for their property. Above market value. So they'll be okay."

Except that they might not want to leave. Her mother didn't. Kara regarded him carefully. Should she say something? On second thought, perhaps not. Better to get through the rest of the date and then say goodbye to Neil for good. She wasn't even sure why he had asked her out. They had absolutely nothing in common.

The server came over. "Can I interest you in dessert?" She was carrying a small menu with sweet offerings.

"None for me, thanks," Kara said. She was stuffed, and she didn't want to prolong the meal.

"Not even to share?" Neil asked in a teasing voice.

Kara shook her head.

He frowned briefly. "Just the check, please."

A few minutes later, they exited the restaurant, Neil continuing his overly solicitous manners. Snow had started to fall, and he insisted on taking her arm as they walked to his car, claiming that he didn't want her to slip.

Kara didn't bother to point out that the pavement was dry and bare and the new flakes weren't even accumulating yet. As he helped her into the vehicle, Kara noticed a police cruiser moving slowly down Main Street. Her heart leaped. Was it Sean? She remembered hearing that he was on patrol tonight.

Neil shut her door and went around to the driver's side. And then they were on their way at last, headed back to her mom's house.

"Thanks for a wonderful dinner," Kara said after Neil pulled into the driveway. She rested her hand on the door handle. "You don't need to help me to the house."

He shifted in his seat as though to get out anyway. "Are you sure?"

Kara opened her car door. "Positive." She forced herself to smile. "See you around. Take care." She put enough finality in her tone to forestall any further conversation—or so she hoped.

"You too," he called as she exited the car.

She sensed him watching her as she climbed the porch steps and fished out her key. But she deliberately unlocked the door and went inside. She was never this rude, but she had the feeling that Neil would take any encouragement she gave him and run with it.

Once inside, she took off her coat and hung it up, then peeked out. Neil backed out of the driveway and started down the street.

A police cruiser crawled toward the house from the opposite direction. It stopped, and so did Neil's car. The two vehicles sat that way for a moment, the drivers obviously talking to each other.

Why was Neil talking to the police? And was it Sean he was speaking to?

A sharp stab of betrayal lanced through Kara. Were Sean and Neil keeping an eye on her—together?

Most nights, Sean didn't mind being out on patrol. His charge was to travel the roads of Castlebridge, keeping an eye on everything and also making a police presence known. Since the outlying areas were rural, he spent the bulk of his time in downtown and the residential neighborhoods. Sometimes he parked for a speed detail, the cruiser a deterrent to those who would race down the hill into town.

He'd been sitting in the cruiser, monitoring traffic on Main Street earlier tonight when he saw Neil Fuller go by. Who could miss the man? His red Audi was enviably eye-catching. As the luxury sedan passed under a streetlight, Sean had spotted Kara sitting in the passenger seat.

Kara and Neil? Two hours later, the thought still gave him a nasty jolt.

He'd never liked Neil. Even in high school, Neil had been insufferable. Arrogant, entitled, and often a royal jerk to those he regarded as beneath him. For a while, Sean had been in that category despite being the police chief's nephew. Since Sean was also a stellar athlete and a good student, he'd often thought that Neil's disdain was more jealousy than anything else. Neil regarded Sean as competition, and what better way to knock him down than to treat him like a loser?

Until the day Sean had had enough and the two boys tussled. The impetus that day had been insults regarding Tiffany, who used to date Neil. The poor girl had been the subject of Neil's snide comments ever since she'd dumped him.

After that Neil had left him alone, and Sean was good with that. But why had Kara been with him tonight? Were they on a date?

He shook his head to clear it. What Kara did with her life was none of his business. He'd forfeited the right to provide input when he had so callously broken up with her.

Sean was lucky that she even gave him the time of day.

Then he asked himself exactly why he cared. Did he still have feelings for her after a decade and a couple of other women in his life? He had to admit that those other relationships hadn't held a candle to the bond he and Kara had shared. They'd been friends first, sharing the same quirky sense of humor. Everything had been more fun with Kara. Taking a ride. Going swimming at the lake. Skiing. Sitting and chatting next to a fireplace or under the stars.

With a melancholy pang, Sean acknowledged the truth. Kara was perfect for him. A true companion, which was rare.

She was gorgeous, no doubt of that. But back in high school, she'd had the kind of simple, natural beauty that adolescent boys didn't always appreciate.

But Sean had appreciated it. Still did. He kicked himself for blowing it back then. Maybe they would have stayed together, been married by now, with a family—

Sean reined in his unruly thoughts. Most teenage romances didn't survive graduation. If he and Kara had been meant to be, they would have stayed together, right?

Maybe. If he hadn't been so stupid and selfish.

Kara's dad had tragically died in a car accident, and naturally that had set her reeling. She'd been withdrawn, depressed, moody.

At first Sean had been constantly at her side, but she hadn't liked that. So he'd withdrawn to give her space—and she'd objected to that, accusing him of not caring. Now he understood. She'd been young, confused, scared, and hurting. And he was just a dumb kid who didn't know what she needed or how to help her.

At the same time, his uncle had pressured him to let her go. Uncle Mark was full of advice about teenage romances, how they usually failed. How it was time to end things with Kara before one of them really got hurt.

To his everlasting shame, he'd listened. And worse, word spread around town that he'd jumped the gun and dated someone else before officially breaking up with Kara.

But Sean had ended his relationship with Kara before he started dating Tiffany. He had desperately wanted to explain to Kara what had really happened, but the rumor mill had been relentless. He was afraid Kara would never believe him. How could he tell her the truth after so many years?

Sean shook his head. From this distance of years, it sounded like an overblown television drama. Tiffany had been grateful for how he'd stood up to Neil, her ex-boyfriend. But Sean and Tiffany had been all wrong for each other. Her beauty and popularity had drawn him, plus the novelty of being a knight in shining armor, but they had nothing in common. Now Tiffany was happily married to someone else. Sean had gone to their wedding and enjoyed every minute of it.

Could he be that happy? Could Kara? He almost allowed himself to hope that her feelings for him weren't completely gone.

He could examine that later, though. He was on the clock and needed to keep his mind on the job.

His route took him near the campus, so he headed in that direction. A leap in his pulse proved that his subconscious knew his plan before he did.

He was going to check on Kara before heading to the college.

Make sure that Neil had delivered her home safely. That was all. He was simply looking out for a friend.

Once on her street, Sean saw the red Audi close to the Foxworth home. Neil was talking through his open driver's side window to an officer in a Castlebridge cruiser in what seemed to be a close conversation.

The sight jolted Sean. He was the only one who was supposed to be on patrol tonight, and he hadn't heard any other officers get called out over the radio.

What were Neil and the officer chatting about? He'd never seen Neil give anyone from the local force more than a cursory greeting.

His instincts told him something was up. And worse, he had a terrible feeling that Kara was right in the middle of it.

Sean was almost upon the two vehicles, which were blocking the street. Since he was coming up on the other cruiser from behind, he could see the license plate number but not the driver.

Neil spotted him and said something to the other officer, then abruptly rolled up his window and accelerated. The other driver did the same.

Professional courtesy required the two officers to stop and chat. But the other car continued up the street as if Sean were invisible.

Peeved at this treatment, Sean picked up the radio and paged the other cruiser.

Nothing. Not a peep in response.

Sean braked to a halt, pondering this odd situation. Now he really knew something was up. Whoever was driving that police car did not want to talk to him.

Rather than chase the officer down and ask what was going on, Sean decided to wait. He could check the log later tonight and find out who had taken the cruiser out. Perturbed, he released the brake and prepared to set off again.

This circuit took him along the back roads, and at one point he passed Nelson Reed's farm. A few lights shone in the farmhouse windows, and he wondered how the man was doing. Even after all these years, the discovery of Angela's body must have been a blow.

Unless he had something to do with it. Sean wanted to reject that thought, but he couldn't. The state police and his uncle seemed to believe it had been an unfortunate accident, but Sean wasn't quite there yet. The lack of a seat belt and the site of the crash both niggled at him. Had the accident been staged somehow? That raised the question of whether Angela had been alive when she crashed into the woods. For her sake, he hoped not.

Anger tightened in his core. He was going to get to the bottom of this whether or not the other officers agreed. He'd need to be careful since going rogue was definitely frowned upon. It could even derail his career plans.

As Sean traveled along the winding rural road, driving slowly to avoid being surprised by any animals in the road, he considered his next steps. Was he willing to put his career at risk for the truth? Many other officers would say no. They would assert that they were hired to follow the leadership and guidance of their chief and the state police.

Insubordination was a firing offense, not something to take lightly. But neither was an unsolved murder. Kara deserved answers about her aunt's death—even if she never spoke to him again.

At the Castlebridge line, Sean turned around and headed back. Then he took a side road that would allow him to circuit the town.

This route led out past Dead Man's Curve, and his anxiety grew as he got closer to the fatal location. How many people had died here? It had a reputation for being deadly, but due to the river valley below and a mountainside above, relocating the road was no easy task.

Maybe now they would finally straighten the curve and make it safer.

Sean pulled over into a wide spot on the shoulder. The interior of the cruiser was hot, so he cracked a window. The night was almost totally silent, the only sound the soughing of wind in the pines.

He studied the place where Angela had gone off the road. Such a narrow opening, a gap framed by large trees on both sides. It almost seemed that someone would have to aim for it.

In the distance, Sean heard a vehicle approaching. The engine had a deep, throaty roar, and the condition of the muffler system was questionable. And by the rate of the increasing noise, he judged the driver was speeding. All they needed was another accident on Dead Man's Curve.

Sean braced himself, ready to flip on his lights and pursue the reckless driver, though he hoped it wouldn't come to that. The driver wouldn't be expecting to see a police cruiser parked here, and he hoped the warning of his presence would suffice.

The vehicle raced down the undulating hills to Dead Man's Curve. Headlights shone in the treetops, and then the vehicle was upon him.

Sean barely had a chance to see that it was a large pickup tricked out with extra headlights on the roof rack. The front license plate was obscured with mud, never a good sign. In response, he flipped the switch, and the blues began to rotate.

The driver of the truck slowed briefly, then sped up and tore past the cruiser as if daring Sean to give chase. Black exhaust belched from the back of the truck like a flag.

Interesting choice. Sean spun the cruiser around and set off after the truck. He really didn't like doing this. Chasing a vehicle was dangerous for him, the other driver, and innocent people on the road.

Sean raced along, driving as fast as was prudent. He was almost to town when he realized that the other driver had vanished. He groaned. The winding road had allowed the truck to disappear onto a side road.

Slowing to the speed limit, Sean continued into town. In his mind's eye, he reviewed everything he'd noticed about the truck, logging details for future use. It was very likely that the truck was local. If so, he would see it again. And maybe have a little talk with the driver.

Instinct had him driving past Kara's house once more. The light was on in Kara's bedroom, and he saw her robed figure pulling the curtains closed. He breathed a sigh of relief. He'd been pretty sure she wasn't in Neil's car when he'd encountered him and the cruiser earlier, and here was the confirmation he needed.

Something flashed in the corner of his eye. He stopped the cruiser to take a closer look. Light was shining from the back of Angela's house.

Had Michelle or Kara left a lamp on? Maybe they thought that would discourage further trespassing.

But then the light moved, exactly as if someone was carrying a flashlight.

Sean didn't hesitate. He put the cruiser into park and shut off the engine. Should he call for backup? He decided to go check it out first.

Armed with his own flashlight, Sean crept around the building, trying to stay out of view. The snow crunched underfoot once or twice, making him wince, and he hoped the sound hadn't been audible to the prowler.

As he went, he peeked into the windows of the house, watching as the light moved from room to room, as though whoever held it was searching for something.

Something in there must be incredibly important for someone to come back and search again. He was also surprised that the Foxworths hadn't changed the locks or installed a security system. But maybe they hadn't been able to get anyone over here yet.

Sean reached the backyard. The light had been stationary in the front of the house for more than a minute, which hopefully meant the intruder would stay put until he got inside.

Once again the back door was ajar, this time with even more damage to the wood. Sean sucked in a breath, angered and appalled. If the prowler didn't find what he wanted in the empty house, would he break into Michelle's house next? The thought made Sean's chest tighten.

Leaving his light off, Sean stepped into the kitchen, moving as quietly as possible. He stood absolutely still, listening with every fiber of his body.

Not a sound, not even a rustle of movement or a footstep.

In a decisive move, he switched on the flashlight and bellowed, "Police! Come out with your hands up!"

The light didn't move.

Sean was about to shout again when someone slammed into his back.

Early the next morning, a series of knocks on the front door roused Kara from sleep. Blinking up at the ceiling, she wondered if she had dreamed it.

No, there it was again, a persistent rapping. She'd better find out who it was before the noise woke her mother. With a sigh, she heaved herself out of bed and threw on a robe, so tired that her fingers fumbled with the sash.

As she shuffled downstairs in her slippers, she tried to remember how late she'd gone to bed. Midnight? One o'clock? Although she'd been mentally and physically exhausted, she had been unable to settle down. She'd puttered around the house, tried to read a book, and finally collapsed into bed, her mind whirring.

The visitor knocked again as she came down the stairs. Practically flying down the rest of the steps, she lunged for the doorknob.

Then her hand stilled. Was it a good idea to just open the door? *Probably not.* Kara moved to the sidelight window and peeked outside to see who it was.

Her heart gave a leap. Sean stood on the porch, hands in his pockets. What was he doing here? Then she noticed the black eye.

Kara opened the door. "What happened to you?"

He cracked a grin. "That's some greeting." Touching his face gingerly, he said, "I had a little run-in with that prowler of yours."

"Prowler of mine?" Kara stepped back. "You'd better come inside. It's freezing."

Sean didn't hesitate to take her up on the invitation. "I'm sorry to wake you," he said as he unzipped his jacket. "I guess I figured you'd be up by now."

"Normally we would be. But with everything . . ." Kara's voice trailed off. She ran a hand through her hair, realizing she hadn't even brushed it before coming downstairs. She was probably a fright.

"It's been a tough few days. I get it." His expression was warm with sympathy. "Why don't you show me the way to the coffee maker, and I'll put on a pot while you get dressed?"

"I can do that," Kara said. She ushered him to the kitchen, where she pointed out everything he needed. Then she rushed upstairs.

Her mother's bedroom door opened a crack. "Is someone here? I thought I heard voices."

"Sean Colton, if you can believe it," Kara said. "And he has a black eye."

Her mom frowned. "A black eye? That doesn't sound good."

"I'm dying to find out how he got it," Kara said. "He's making coffee, so come on down when you're ready."

"I'll join you both in a few minutes."

Kara hurried to her room, where she quickly washed her face, brushed her teeth, and dressed in jeans and a sweater, then pulled on thick, woolly socks. After combing her hair and adding a touch of lip gloss, she was ready to go. She didn't want Sean to think she'd tried too hard, so she decided to skip any more makeup.

Down in the kitchen, Sean was taking mugs out of the cupboard. "Coffee is ready," he said, his gaze sweeping over her attire.

Was she imagining the approval in his eyes? Or in his one good eye at least. Kara chided herself. Why did she care?

"I'd love a cup," she said, moving toward the refrigerator. She retrieved the milk. "Are you hungry? I'm going to make omelets." She reached for an egg carton, cheese, and ham. Fresh mushrooms, green pepper, and onion were next.

"That should be quite an omelet," Sean said, taking in the assortment of ingredients. "How can I refuse?" He grinned. "I still remember your kitchen-sink sandwiches." That had been his nickname for the massive concoctions she'd put together back in high school. Everything but the kitchen sink.

"I do too," she said. It had become a challenge to surprise and delight him with unusual combinations.

Her mother wandered into the kitchen, dressed in slacks and a sweater. "Is that coffee I smell?" She nodded at their guest. "Good morning. How have you been?"

Busy dicing vegetables, Kara breathed out a sigh of relief. She had wondered how her mother would react to a police officer's morning visit. She seemed to be taking it in stride, perhaps because Sean was dressed in street clothing.

"I'm fine. How are you?" Sean handed her mom a mug of coffee. "It probably isn't as good as yours, but I hope it will do."

Her mother added milk and took a sip. "It's perfect." She sat at the table. "I'm going to watch you two work, if you don't mind."

"You can run the toaster," Kara said to Sean. "Bread is in the bread box." She pointed to the vintage stainless steel container on the counter.

Soon vegetables were sizzling in butter, and Kara was beating eggs. Between rounds of toast, Sean grated cheese into a bowl. Her mom turned on the radio, and instrumental Christmas music filled the air.

As Kara poured golden eggs into the pan, she realized something. She was enjoying this. The warm kitchen. The delicious aromas teasing her nose. Her mother's smile. Sean's company.

She paused in her task. Maybe she enjoyed having Sean here

because it felt familiar, like muscle memory. She caught his eye, and a hot blush heated her face. Or maybe it wasn't just familiarity at all.

She couldn't deny it. Sean Colton was a very attractive man, despite the shiner he was sporting. The years had filled out his face and physique, deepened his voice, and given his movements the weight of self-assurance and maturity.

Hoping desperately that he hadn't also gained the ability to read her mind, she refocused on the frying pan.

Somehow, despite the distraction, she served up fluffy eggs mixed with finely diced ham and vegetables and oozing with melted Vermont cheddar. Perhaps her best omelet ever.

The silence at the breakfast table confirmed her opinion.

After devouring his omelet and three slices of toast, Sean sat back with a groan. "That's the best thing I've eaten in weeks." He patted his midsection. "Really hit the spot."

"It is good," her mom agreed. She'd eaten almost as much as Sean.

Kara was warmed by the compliments. "I like to cook, but it's not much fun for one."

"Tell me about it," her mother said, echoed by Sean.

Everyone laughed.

"I guess we're all in the same boat," Sean said, cradling his mug in both hands. "Except I have a cat. And judging by his demands, he counts as a roommate."

Her mom's face lit with interest. "What's his name? I've been thinking about getting a cat. I lost my last one about three years ago, and I haven't had the heart to adopt again."

"I guess you could say he adopted me," Sean said. "His name is Bandit, and I caught him stealing my sandwich while I was raking the yard for Miss Eleanor."

"How is your landlady?" her mom asked.

"She's doing well for eighty-five." He grinned. "She's still spoiling me with delicious treats." Her mom laughed. "I'm glad to hear it." She glanced at the kitchen clock, then pushed back from the table. "If you'll excuse me, I've got a couple of errands before I head to the library." To Kara, she said, "I'm working until six this evening."

"I'll make dinner," Kara said. "Any suggestions?"

"There's frozen spaghetti sauce with meatballs in the freezer. But go ahead and eat when you get hungry. Don't wait for me." Her mother turned to Sean. "Nice to see you. By the way, where did you get that beautiful black eye?"

Sean touched the skin around his eye. "I had a run-in with a bad guy. Comes with the territory. It was nice to see you as well."

After her mom left the kitchen, Kara and Sean sat quietly for a moment.

Once she heard her mother's footsteps moving around upstairs, she said in a low voice, "Tell me what really happened. I'm guessing it's something to do with next door." She tipped her head in the direction of Angela's home.

Sean rose. "Before I get into it, want a refill?" He reached for her mug.

Kara handed it over. While he got the coffee, she stacked their dirty plates, leaving them to one side. As she settled back into her chair, her cell phone bleeped with a text.

It was from Neil. *Had a great time last night. Do it again soon?*

How should she respond? Kara had no interest in going out with Neil again. But saying such a thing bluntly in a text seemed wrong. And there was Tiffany's warning too. What was that about? Did she know something about Neil that Kara didn't?

Sean placed her mug in front of her, and she hastily flipped her phone over. Hopefully he hadn't seen the message, although she didn't know why she should care. She and Sean were long over, right?

As he sat on the other side of the table, he said, "I surprised another intruder in Angela's place last night."

Her heart skipped a beat. It must have been Sean talking to Neil then. But rather than confront him about that, she asked, "You were in the neighborhood?" She added a splash of milk to the mug and stirred, pretending not to be too interested in his answer.

Red burned across his cheekbones. "Yes. I was on patrol last night, and I noticed a light on. I thought I'd better check it out."

"And?" Kara picked up her mug and sipped, her eyes never leaving his face.

Sean shifted in his chair. "At first I thought you had left a light on. But after I saw it moving around, I got out of my cruiser and circled the house. They broke in again through the back." His expression was quizzical. "I take it you didn't change the locks or install a security system yet?"

Kara frowned, feeling defensive. "We called the locksmith yesterday, but he said that he was backed up and it would be a couple of days. I had no idea the intruder would come back and so soon."

Sean tapped the table. "I'd call again and tell him to move you up the list. Two break-ins in as many days? That's not acceptable."

"You're telling me," she muttered.

Light footsteps came down the stairs. Her mother poked her head into the room. "I'm heading out. See you later."

After they chorused goodbyes, Sean said, "Do you want me to call the locksmith? Sometimes a nudge from the police works wonders."

Kara hated that her first reaction was reluctance. Did she really want Sean to get involved with installing the locks next door? "No, I can handle it. I'll call this morning." She studied his black eye again. "Okay, you noticed someone broke in. Then what?"

"I announced my presence, and the intruder jumped me and started pummeling." Sean touched his eye again. "I haven't been caught off guard like that in years. I must be slipping."

She felt terrible that Sean had been hurt, but it was more than that. What if he'd suffered a worse injury? Her stomach clenched. "That's awful," she finally managed.

His smile was wry. "Don't worry. I defended myself. Then the guy took off. I thought about calling for backup, but by the time I got outside, he was gone. I heard a vehicle start up on the next street. So I never even saw it."

"I wonder what they want," Kara said. "The first time you can attribute to someone taking advantage of an empty house. But twice? No, they must think Angela had something important."

"That's what I think too." Sean paused. "I wish I knew what was going on in her life before she disappeared."

"Me too," she said. "I don't believe it's a coincidence that they broke in after her car was found. They had ten years to get in there and dig around." Had the intruder assumed that Angela had run away with whatever it was? "Did you find anything in her car?"

"Nothing out of the ordinary," he replied. "A handbag with a few personal items. Once they make a ruling, we'll release her personal effects."

"Will that be soon?" Kara asked. She would have loved to see Angela's purse and other belongings, things that connected her to her beloved aunt, even though they probably weren't in very good condition after so much time.

Sean shrugged. "Hard to say. I can tell the chief and the state police that you'd like to have her personal effects as soon as possible."

"Would you?" Kara heard the pleading sound in her own voice and bit her lip, annoyed. She cleared her throat. "I'd appreciate it."

He glanced at the clock. "I hate to say this, but I need to get going soon. Want to take a look at the house before I go?"

"Yes, I do," she said. "But before we go over, let me call the locksmith again."

This time, after hearing about the second break-in, the company agreed to dispatch a van immediately. "They'll meet us there," she told Sean after she hung up.

A few minutes later, Sean led the way to Angela's house and showed Kara the back door.

Kara's heart squeezed. What a violation for someone to literally force their way into a home. "How bad is it inside?"

"I didn't get a chance to check it out," Sean said. "And the lights were out. Want to go in?"

"No," Kara said honestly. "But I suppose we'd better." She or her mother needed to check it out in case something was missing or damaged. Not only would they need to take care of it, but they'd also need to file an insurance claim on both incidents. But insurance wouldn't restore their sense of security.

She followed Sean into the kitchen, releasing her held breath when she saw it was exactly as she had left it. "Nothing new here."

The rest of the house was the same.

"He must have just gotten in when I surprised him," Sean said. "Or should I say, he surprised me."

The rumble of tires in the driveway announced the locksmith's arrival.

"Want me to stay?" Sean offered.

"I'll be fine," Kara said. "But thank you."

After escorting him outside, she watched Sean stride to his truck, his long legs eating up the distance. Why did she feel so conflicted? Every time she found herself relaxing into the easy friendship they had once shared, doubts arose, making her pull back. Were they a knee-jerk reaction to the past, a subconscious warning that he was untrustworthy?

His betrayal all those years ago had cut deeply, partly because she'd still been grieving the death of her father. She had been vulnerable, needy, and a mess.

Her rational adult mind told her that he'd been a kid—and so had she. Teenage romances didn't last forever. They probably would have broken up after they graduated. Her father's death had hastened the process, and she really couldn't blame Sean for his reaction. He had been in over his head.

Could Kara trust Sean now? Or was relying on him still a recipe for heartbreak?

"Are you ready to show me around?" the locksmith asked, startling her out of her reverie.

"You bet," Kara said. "Come with me."

After the locksmith left, Kara returned to her mother's house. As she sipped another cup of coffee, she wondered how to spend the rest of the day. She still had Christmas shopping to do as well as a new book she could read by the fire, but neither of those appealed to her right now.

Not when she'd rather seek answers about her aunt's death. Kara decided that talking to Nelson Reed was the next obvious step. She would drive out to the farm without calling first. She'd be able to tell a lot about his true state of mind from his initial reaction.

After some internal debate, Kara grabbed the card she'd found at Angela's to show the farmer, but she left the covered bridge embroidery behind. Yes, Angela's will had left it to Nelson. Kara would give it to him eventually, but she wanted to feel him out first. Besides, she wasn't quite ready to let go of it.

As Kara drove out to the dairy farm, she checked the rearview mirror frequently, keeping an eye out for the black pickup. She'd put on a brave face for her mother, but the encounter had scared her badly.

Now there had been a second break-in at Angela's. What was next, an invasion of her mom's home? And what exactly were they looking for? A review of Angela's will had affirmed that her aunt hadn't owned anything especially valuable. No jewelry or gold coins or rare artwork. There was the house and some money in a bank account, and that was it.

Kara wondered if they should install a security system at her mother's house as well. The cameras and sensors hadn't been that pricey, and they could monitor the situation from their cell phones, which was very handy.

On impulse, she pulled over on the side of the road to check. She actually had a signal here, and she quickly opened the app to check the security system.

All was well, and the rooms were quiet in the sun. If someone attempted to break in again, an alarm would go off that would summon her and the police. She'd chosen the silent setting so that the person wouldn't realize that law enforcement was on the way.

Kara put away her phone and set off again, wondering how often she would be tempted to check the cameras to make sure everything was all right. She was sure it would take a while to get over the trauma of the invasion.

She arrived at Nelson's dairy farm. *Here we go.* Would Nelson have answers—or would visiting him only raise more questions?

Kara pulled up the long drive and parked near the house, which was a classic Vermont farmhouse with a main section and an ell attached to the rear. Farmhouse kitchens, the heart of the home, were usually located in the ell, so she parked near that entrance. Straight ahead was a large red barn, and other outbuildings were scattered beyond it. A white pickup and a one-ton dump truck were parked near the barn.

During very cold weather, the cows stayed inside. As Kara got out of her car, she heard mooing from the barn. She idly wondered if cows got cabin fever as humans did.

Kara crossed the side porch sheltering the back door and knocked.

No answer, although a dog began to bark.

Putting her hands to her face, she peeked inside. The aforementioned dog, an old golden retriever, trotted into the kitchen, toenails sliding on the hardwood floor. The animal came right up to the window and woofed, almost deafeningly. If Nelson didn't hear his dog, he must be away from home or somewhere on the property.

"Can I help you?" someone asked in a low, rough voice right behind Kara.

She jumped and whirled around, hand on her chest, to see a burly man dressed in overalls and a barn jacket, a wool hat pulled low over his brow. His broad face was set in a scowl, and he hadn't shaved recently.

"You're not Nelson," Kara said. She remembered the farmer as being tall and handsome, with a shock of brown hair and gentle eyes. This man was anything but gentle. Kara looked past him to her car. Would he try to stop her if she bolted?

He laughed, revealing crooked, yellowed teeth. "Good one. I'm Roy. I help out around here."

"Is Nelson here?" Kara asked, noticing the tremble in her voice. She bit her lip, hating to let Roy know that he intimidated her.

After studying her for a long, fraught moment, he said, "I think he's out in the sugar shack. Should be back soon. You can wait for him in the house or walk over and talk to him."

Kara didn't want to wait in Nelson's house, especially with Roy hanging around. "I'll go find him."

She thankfully didn't have to ask which building he meant, because she'd been to more than one sugar shack. These distinctive buildings were where maple syrup was made, and they all had a cupola on top to allow steam from boiling sap to escape. She did wonder why Nelson would be in the shack now, since maple syrup season wasn't until late February, but she didn't bother to ask Roy. She was too eager to get away from him.

Glad she'd worn boots, Kara made her way across the farmyard. The route to the sugar shack had been cleared by a snow blower, so she wasn't wading through deep snow. She passed the barn, where cows mooed again, perhaps sensing her presence. "Sorry, ladies," she said. "I'm not here to feed you." She pictured them in their stalls, big heads swinging as they munched on bales of hay and troughs of grain. She loved cows, with their big brown eyes and soft, broad noses.

The wind whipped across the open fields the moment she stepped out of the shelter of the barn, sending a spray of fine snow into her face. Kara hunched her shoulders and kept going, her gaze fixed on her destination. The buzz of a snowmobile echoed through the woods ahead, but she couldn't see the machine or the rider. Was that Nelson, doing rounds of his extensive property? What if he'd left the sugar shack?

Then she'd return to the car and go home.

Kara was over halfway there, so she trudged on, feeling as if she would never arrive. At last she made it to the shack, which was located in a cleared area at the edge of the woods.

She paused, feeling apprehensive about talking to Nelson. She really didn't know the farmer. She had vague memories of him at dinners and holidays with her aunt, but she hadn't talked to him beyond the usual niceties. She'd been a teenager and more interested in people her own age, not the adults around her who seemed ancient to her young eyes.

What if Nelson had something to do with what happened to her aunt? Her hand stilled on the door latch. *There's no proof of that.* With that fortifying thought, she pressed the latch and stepped inside. The shack was bigger than she'd expected, and it was dark, with only a little light entering through the small windows on the sides. In the spring, double doors on both ends would stand open to accept the sap and loads of firewood that were needed for the operation. She vaguely recalled that it took forty gallons of sap to make one gallon of syrup.

"Nelson?" Kara called.

No answer.

She didn't want to venture to the other side of the building to see if he was in the adjacent shed. It was too cold. When she called out again and there was still no response, she decided to return to the house. Roy must have been mistaken about Nelson's whereabouts. Or maybe he had been to the shack and left already.

Her hand was on the door latch when she heard the creak of floorboards. Before she could turn to see what had made the noise, a smothering cloth was suddenly draped over her head. Burlap, judging by the weave and the dusty smell of grain.

Strong arms gripped her body, trapping her arms and lifting her off the floor.

Kara began to kick. "Help me!" she screamed, but the cloth muffled her voice.

The man didn't let her go. Grunting, he carried her through the building and then pushed her forward.

Her arms flailed. *What is happening?* She landed hard on her knees, the shock traveling up her spine.

A door slammed, reverberating in the frame, and a dead bolt slid into place.

Sobbing in pain and shock, Kara tore the burlap off her head. She was trapped in a dark, windowless room.

After what Sean had thought was a very enjoyable breakfast with Kara and her mother, he had been firmly rebuffed at Angela's house. *Kara doesn't trust me.* The truth nestled in his gut, unsettling him.

As he drove the side streets toward home after stopping at the grocery store, he mulled over the situation. Was it because of their shared past? No arguments there. He *had* proved himself untrustworthy. He still squirmed when he thought about his actions so long ago. Or was her distrust a result of Angela's death?

In that case, Sean didn't blame Kara for being wary of him or anyone else. The police department hadn't prioritized finding her aunt in the first place, and now Kara had been plagued by break-ins and threats since the discovery of her aunt's body. Maybe she didn't feel she could trust the police—or anyone who had known her aunt.

He'd probably feel the same way. Slightly reassured by this conclusion, Sean pulled into his driveway. His first task was to check on Miss Eleanor, which he did several times a day.

Miss Eleanor answered immediately when he knocked on the back door. "Good timing," she said, her blue eyes bright with welcome. "I just pulled an applesauce cake out of the oven." Then she peered at him. "What happened to you?"

His black eye. Of course she'd noticed it. How could she not? "I bumped into a doorjamb in the middle of the night," he fibbed, knowing how lame it sounded.

But Miss Eleanor nodded, seeming to accept his explanation.

He followed the slender figure of his landlady into the house, pausing in the mudroom to slip out of his boots and take off his jacket. The old-fashioned kitchen was cozy, warmed by Miss Eleanor's baking. In addition to the cake, she had made several batches of chocolate chip cookies.

"Those are for the church bake sale," she said, pouring him a cup of coffee. She winked. "But I won't tell if you steal one."

"Stealing church cookies? I don't know about that." Sean reached for one and broke it in half. It was still warm and oozing chocolate.

He sat at the table and allowed her to fuss over him, serving him the coffee and a plate with a generous square of cake. Although Miss Eleanor needed help with heavy work, like in the yard or washing floors, she prided herself on staying active.

She cut herself a piece of cake. "Got to keep myself busy. I garden in the summer, and I bake in the winter."

"And we all benefit," Sean said. The applesauce cake was moist and sweet, flavored with delicious spices. "I think this is my favorite thing you make."

Miss Eleanor laughed. "Last week it was the chocolate crazy cake."

"That was good too," he said around a mouthful. Crazy cake was a recipe from the Depression era that omitted eggs, butter, and milk, but it was surprisingly tasty.

"I heard the bad news," Miss Eleanor said without preamble. Her expression was troubled. "A sad, sad thing."

"It certainly is," Sean said, guessing that she was talking about Angela Foxworth. "A shock to all concerned."

"That poor family." Miss Eleanor sighed. "First Miles and now this." She took a sip of coffee, then said, "George and Miles were great friends, you know." George was her late husband. He and Miles had both been architects.

Sean felt a quickening of interest. "Did they work together?" He knew George had owned his own firm.

"No," Miss Eleanor answered. "If George hadn't been winding down, he would have hired him in a minute, though. He said Miles was extremely talented."

"I'm sure he was." Sean tucked the compliment away to share with Kara later. George had been an award-winning designer of buildings all over New England, so his opinion meant something.

After falling silent for a moment, Miss Eleanor said, "I was so shocked when Miles had that accident. He'd been to visit George a day or two before. They had quite the discussion."

His interest was definitely piqued now. "What was it about?"

"I don't know all the details—I'm afraid I used to let a lot of what George said go over my head—but it had something to do with the Fuller Mill job."

The renovation of the Fuller Mill had been a high-profile, multimillion-dollar project that blended private and public funds.

"Something wrong with the plans?" Sean asked cautiously. The last thing he wanted to do was carelessly throw accusations around. The Fullers had a great deal of influence in town, and several people who crossed them had found themselves seeking new employment or moving away. It was all very covert, so no one could prove what was really happening.

Miss Eleanor pursed her lips. "Something like that. A mismatch between specs and the actual job."

A thrill ran down Sean's spine. He fully understood the subtext. Benedict Fuller had cut corners, probably by using cheaper materials or methods than had been promised. It happened all the time, and since Fuller still owned the mill complex, he wasn't likely to report on himself.

"What was Miles going to do about it?" he asked.

"I'm not sure," Miss Eleanor said. "I know he was very troubled, but to report the problems probably would have meant losing his job. The mill project was a large one for his employer."

Would Miles have blown the whistle if he had lived? Was it a coincidence that he died a day or two later in a car accident?

Sean shook his head. He couldn't operate this way, seeing conspiracies where there were probably none. And now wasn't the time to think about Miles Foxworth. He needed to uncover answers about Miles's sister, Angela.

"I wish I knew more," Miss Eleanor said. "But like I said, I wasn't really paying attention. Conflicts between architects and clients happen all the time."

But had this one risen to the level of murder? Sean certainly hoped not. Another question was whether Miles had told Angela about the situation. He remembered that she'd worked for Fuller's attorney, Walter Hill. Had the corruption gone beyond that particular construction project? Fuller had his finger in a lot of pies, and his attorney was probably privy to most of them. Especially since attorney-client privilege would apply, shielding both men.

The one thing Sean knew for certain was that Benedict Fuller's companies generated a lot of money.

And with big money often came big temptations.

After his conversation with Miss Eleanor, Sean decided to talk to Nelson. Fully aware that he was acting without permission, Sean drove out to the dairy farm before reporting for duty. If pressed, he would use the excuse that both he and Miss Eleanor needed maple syrup. Although Nelson sold most of his stock to stores, he kept some around for locals.

On the way out to the farm, Sean kept an eye out for the black pickup truck. If the driver was local, he would spot the truck sooner or later. If he wasn't, then it wasn't Sean's problem.

Sean also mulled over the Angela Foxworth case, wondering how to broach it with the chief. He would have to file a report about being attacked the previous night. He couldn't hide his black eye, and besides, he had been well within bounds to investigate the mysterious light.

And he also needed to find out who was driving the other cruiser. That was a little trickier because the last thing he wanted to do right now was make waves. No, it would be best if he minimized conflict while working on his exit plan. Getting in trouble or even suspended would not help his application to the state police.

He gritted his teeth at the thought, which went against the grain. He believed in being honest. Playing political games to get ahead was not his style.

The dairy farm loomed up ahead, and Sean slowed. He eased up the long drive. When he spotted a familiar sedan, he braked sharply, his tires shooting up a spray of snow.

What was Kara doing here?

Unless she was buying syrup, he had a very good idea. She was talking to Nelson about her aunt. Which she had every right to do, he admitted. But still, the idea made Sean uneasy.

Sean pressed the gas again, rolling forward into a better spot so as not to block the driveway. He shut off the engine and hopped out, then headed to the side door.

No answer to his knock except the barking of Nelson's dog. He peered into the kitchen, but no one was in there.

Where was Kara? Sean studied the farmyard and the assorted outbuildings. Could she be in the barn? Sometimes Nelson gave visitors a tour. He enjoyed showing off his herd of beautiful Jersey cows.

He zipped his jacket and went toward the barn, fully expecting to find Kara and Nelson inside. Two rows of curious cows stared at him, and there were no other humans in sight. "Sorry, ladies," he said, backing away. "Didn't mean to interrupt your meal."

As he stepped out of the barn, he almost bumped right into Nelson Reed. "There you are," he said. "I'm Sean Colton."

Nelson, dressed in warm outdoor clothing, rocked back on his heels slightly, regarding Sean with narrowed eyes. "I know who you are. How can I help you?"

Taken off guard by the farmer's brusque tone, Sean gave a little laugh. "Well, I was here to buy some syrup, but tell me. Where is Kara Foxworth?" He pointed at the sedan. "That's her car."

Nelson turned to study the car. "That's what I was wondering myself. Have you seen Roy around?"

"Roy?" Sean shook his head. "I haven't seen anyone. Unless he's somewhere in the barn."

"Maybe the milk room." Nelson pushed past Sean and opened the door.

Without waiting for an invitation, Sean followed the farmer back inside. Nelson paused to check on a couple of cows, then continued through the stall area to the rear. They entered a room filled with stainless steel equipment and tanks. Everything was sparkling clean.

"They're not here," Sean said. "Any idea where they could be?"

"Did you check the house?" Nelson asked. "She might have gone inside to wait for me."

"I don't think so. No one answered my knock." Sean smiled. "Well, no one other than your dog."

From the creases that appeared between the farmer's brows, Sean guessed that Nelson was starting to get worried. The wrinkles stood out sharply in his smooth face. Nelson had to be in his late fifties, but he was fit and strong and appeared quite youthful. Only a few threads of gray lightened his mop of dark hair.

"Let's check," Nelson said.

Sean followed as they left the barn and went to the house. When Nelson opened the door, the dog bolted outside, barking. She began to trot across the farmyard, nose to the ground, feathery tail wagging.

"Where are you going, Sadie?" Nelson called. He whistled, but the dog didn't respond. He sighed. "Hold on. I'm going to look inside."

Nelson returned a moment later. "Nope."

The way the dog was sniffing around suggested she was tracking something—or someone.

"Maybe Sadie knows where she is," Sean suggested.

Nelson went after the dog. Sean decided to stick with the pair. Kara wasn't in the house or the barn. Would she take a walk through the fields? He noticed a smaller building with a surrounding pen—a chicken coop.

"Do you think she went to visit the chickens?" Sean asked as he caught up to Nelson.

"No idea," Nelson said. His mouth was set in a grim line. "We can check."

But Sadie trotted right past the coop. She veered onto a path that led toward the woods and Nelson's sugar shack.

To their left, the grind of an engine caught Sean's attention. A burly man with his hat pulled low over his eyes was using a small tractor to push snow away from a barn entrance.

"Let me ask Roy if he's seen her," Nelson said. He strode across the snow toward the man, Sadie at his side.

Sean waited. From where he stood, he could see Roy shake his head. He said a few words, and then Nelson turned and made his way back.

"What did he say?" Sean asked.

"He said he told her that she could wait in the house." Nelson grimaced. "Or talk to me in the sugar shack."

The sugar shack wasn't that far. Would Kara have chosen to take a walk rather than wait in comfort in a warm house? But she wasn't inside the farmhouse, so she must have.

"I was in the shack earlier but not for long," Nelson said. "Then I went out to check the stand of sugar maples. The storms we've been having caused some damage."

"Sorry to hear that," Sean said. He noticed the dog was now on the path to the shack. "Sadie must think she went that way."

The two men continued to trail the dog, Sean's anxiety growing with every footstep. He scanned the snowy path for signs of Kara's footprints. But the snow was frozen solid into ridges left by tractor tires.

Then he spotted a small footprint off to one side, where the snow was still powdery. "Look. She did come this way."

Nelson glanced over. "You're right. That print certainly doesn't belong to me or Roy." He lifted a rubber boot. "Size twelve here."

Gripped by a new sense of urgency, Sean picked up his pace. "Is there heat in the shack?" he asked. If Kara was inside, she was probably freezing by now. He didn't allow himself to think about the possibility that she wasn't there.

"I'm afraid not," Nelson said. "We have to fire up the evaporator. Plenty of heat then."

Sean could attest to that. He'd been inside many a shack during sugaring season. "I'm sorry, but I'm really worried." He started to run, not caring if the farmer kept up or not.

When they arrived at the shack, Sadie began to bark again. Sean reached past her and unlatched the big door. With a whine, the retriever bolted inside.

The dog ran through the long building to the rear, where she skidded to a stop. Leaping up, she scratched at the plain wooden door, continuing to whine.

With a lurch of his heart, Sean saw a familiar handbag sitting on the floor near the door. Then Sean saw the engaged dead bolt on the door. In a lightning flash, he knew. Someone had trapped Kara inside.

Without asking for permission, Sean wrenched the thick bolt aside. "Kara," he called, unlatching the door. "Kara!" He yanked open the door to let in more light. Using his leg, he held back a whining Sadie, who tried to push past.

Kara was seated on the floor, arms wrapped around her knees.

Sean's heart lurched painfully, then began to pound. This reaction—mind-numbering fear mingled with blessed relief—told him something. He was head over heels for Kara. Again.

Kara was almost overwhelmed by a rush of relief when she saw Sean standing in the doorway of her prison. She'd been so afraid that the other man had returned, the one who had thrown a sack over her head and tossed her around like a heap of rubbish.

Despite all her doubts about Sean, she knew with deep certainty that he hadn't been her attacker.

Then she saw Nelson Reed crowding behind him, holding his dog's collar, and shrank back. Had it been Nelson? But why would he do such a thing?

"It's okay," Sean said, walking slowly into the room as though not to startle her. "Are you hurt?" He hunkered down beside her, his face creased with concern.

"Nothing serious," she said. "I feel a bit sore, and I'm probably bruised. I landed on the floor pretty hard when he pushed me."

Sean turned to Nelson, who was still standing in the doorway. "Any idea who did this?" His tone was hard and authoritative.

Kara was glad the question wasn't directed at her.

Nelson stepped into the room, clearly upset. "I don't know. And I'm really shocked that something like this would happen." He pulled off his cap and ran a hand through his hair. "It's only me and Roy here. I can talk to him, but he's worked for me for years. I can't imagine ... " He moved closer to Kara, his eyes softening. "I'm so sorry about this. I can't tell you how much." His voice was anguished.

Kara stared at Nelson, taking in his familiar features. Why had she waited so long to come see him? They'd both loved Angela. And even though she was sitting in his sugar shack, she couldn't believe that he had something to do with the attack.

"I'll be fine," she said. "But what a way to meet again, huh?"

Sadie barged through the narrow opening and ran over to Kara, sniffing at her and then licking her cheek.

Kara laughed, trying to fend her off.

"Sorry about that," Nelson said, whistling to the dog. "I'll put her outside." He grabbed her collar and urged her along to the main room.

Sean turned back to Kara. With gentle hands, he felt along her limbs, asking if they hurt, seeing if anything was broken as well as he could through the winter clothes. "Can you stand up? Let's get you somewhere warm." He put his arm around her shoulders and eased her off the floor and into an upright position.

She took a tentative step, feeling an ache in her hip and along her thigh, but thankfully she could move. "I can walk okay." She tried to laugh. "Maybe like a turtle, but I'll make it."

"It's quite a distance to the house if you're not feeling up to it," Sean said dubiously.

Nelson returned. "Wait here. I'll get the snowmobile." He practically ran from the room.

"Lean on me," Sean commanded. He put a strong arm around her, practically carrying her as they moved along.

Kara took the opportunity to nestle close into his warmth, enjoying the sense of safety he gave her.

"How are you doing?" he asked after a moment, his eyes and voice full of tenderness.

Her heart skipped a beat. Was she imagining it, or did he still have feelings for her? And if so, how did she feel about that? To cover her confusion, she said, "I'm doing okay." She gave a little laugh. "You carrying me along is really helping."

Out in the main room, several folding chairs were placed along a wall. Sean helped her to one, then sat in the adjacent seat. He leaned close, brow furrowed as he studied her face. Back in police officer mode. "Tell me what happened. Every detail you remember." He glanced around the quiet building. "Why did you come out to this shack?"

"Roy thought Nelson was here," Kara answered, then took Sean through her entire visit to the farm. "I didn't see the man who attacked me, so I can't give you any details about him," she concluded. "All I noticed was the burlap sack, the feel of it, the dusty smell."

Sean had been silent, listening intently. "I know you didn't see the attacker, but do you have any thoughts on his height or weight?"

Kara closed her eyes, putting herself back into the memory. She started to tremble as the images flashed into her mind. Then she felt Sean's big, warm hand wrap around hers and sighed at the sheer relief of his comforting touch. "He wasn't terribly tall. Not like Nelson." That realization brought another spike of relief. She hadn't believed that Nelson would do such a thing, and this confirmed it. "But he was bulky. Strong. He lifted me up like it was nothing."

"Good," Sean said. He squeezed her hand. "That's all good." He paused. "Was he similar in size to Roy?"

Kara compared the hired hand to the man in her memory. "Maybe. But would he really do that to me? It wasn't like Nelson wouldn't find out about it." Then a squeak of dismay escaped. "Unless he was planning to leave me here. Or worse. And he didn't care if Nelson found out because he was going to take off." Despite the pain in her hip, she found herself jumping up, ready to run. Had Roy—or whoever—planned to *kill* her?

"Calm down," Sean said, taking her by the shoulders. "I promise we're going to get to the bottom of this."

Kara sagged against him. "I sure hope so. I've been attacked, threatened, and knocked down." Hot tears burned her eyes. "What is going on? Why is this happening?"

"I don't know," he said. "But I believe it has something to do with your aunt."

Startled, she gazed up into his face, noting the sincerity in his eyes. "Me too. For one thing, somebody believes that she had something important in her home. Otherwise, why break in twice?" She gritted her teeth. "Obviously they want me to back off and not try to figure it out. Fat chance."

"You need to—" His tone held a note of warning. But before he could say anything else, the sound of a snowmobile approaching grew louder. Nelson was back.

"Should I report this incident to the police? I mean, officially?" Kara asked. But then she thought better of it. "Probably not. I don't want to make trouble for Nelson." She could imagine the fallout if people learned that she'd been attacked at his farm. He'd lose all his customers. If she thought he was guilty, she would do it immediately. But at the moment she believed he was innocent.

"Are you sure?" Sean searched her face. "You don't have to decide right now. I'm a witness, and so is Nelson."

Kara nodded. "I'll think about it."

They both turned as Nelson opened the main door.

The farmer's face was red from the wind. He pulled off a thick glove and scratched his nose. "Sean, you're going to want to see this. There are fresh snowmobile tracks on my property, ones that don't belong to my machine. Proof that someone else was here. The tracks are on the far side of the sugar shack and go through the woods. They don't go to the house."

Kara felt a jolt as a memory surfaced. "I heard a snowmobile somewhere out here." If her attacker had arrived—and left—by snowmobile through the woods, she realized he couldn't have been Roy. She'd left him at Nelson's home. But how had her assailant known she was here? The timing was certainly strange.

"I'll check them out," Sean said. "But let's get Kara to the house first."

Outside the sugar shack, Nelson hopped onto the snowmobile, and Sean helped Kara get settled into the seat behind. After making sure she was ready, the farmer drove slowly down the path to the farmhouse.

Kara was glad for the ride, but at the same time she wanted it to end. Every sway and bump of the machine made her hip and shoulder hurt.

Sean trotted along behind them, reaching the house soon after they did.

She noticed that he wasn't even huffing for air. *He must really be in shape.*

Nelson had brought Sadie back to the house, and the dog greeted Kara with whines and leaps of joy when she entered the warm kitchen.

"What a sweet girl," Kara said, patting the dog's silky head.

"She's the one who found you. Have a seat," Nelson said, indicating a rocking chair next to the woodstove. He opened the stove door and poked the coals before adding another log. "I'll send Roy to check out the barns in case someone's wandering around on foot. We'll be right back."

"Will you be okay here alone?" Sean asked, his eyes dark with worry.

Kara eased herself into the rocker, her loyal companion flopping at her feet. She laughed. "I'll be fine. Sadie will take good care of me."

With one last concerned glance, Sean followed Nelson out, and a moment later, she heard the snowmobile start up again.

As the noise faded into the distance, Kara leaned her head back against the rocker, using her toe to gently push the chair.

Fearful thoughts and speculations clamored in her mind, but she forced them away, trying to focus on the moment. Heat emanating from the stove, where wood was crackling. The dog's soft bulk leaning against her shins. The leftover aromas of coffee and bacon from breakfast. She closed her eyes and tried to release the tension racking her body. Now that the adrenaline rush was gone, she was exhausted.

The kitchen doorknob rattled, and Kara sat bolt upright, her movement disturbing the dog, who groaned. She'd dozed off. Were they back already? She hadn't heard the snowmobile return.

"Uh, sorry, miss." It was Roy, the hired hand. He hesitated halfway through the door. "I didn't mean to bother you."

At the sound of his voice, Sadie gave a low woof, then settled down when she recognized the new arrival.

"Nelson and Sean will be right back if that's who you're looking for," Kara said. "Sadie and I are relaxing." She prayed he would take the hint and leave.

But Roy shuffled his feet in indecision before coming fully inside and closing the door behind him. "It's lunchtime, and I always eat in here. My stuff is in the fridge."

A knot formed in Kara's stomach at the man's intrusion, but she didn't bother to protest further. Nelson and Sean should be back any minute, and her canine protector was right here. Surely Sadie would bite if he got too close. Kara would tell the dog to attack—and hope she listened, in spite of knowing Roy.

Kara watched closely as Roy unzipped and hung up his coat, then removed his wool cap, running his fingers through his greasy hair. Next he kicked off his thick boots before moving to the sink to wash his hands. The attacker had definitely been taller than Roy but not as tall as Nelson. He'd been strong and bulky, though, like Roy. Able to pick her up as if she were a feather.

Moving slowly, seemingly without a care in the world, Roy opened the refrigerator door and retrieved a paper bag. Then he went to the stove and switched on the burner under a kettle, shaking it first to be sure it held water.

"Why did you send me to the sugar shack?" Kara bit her lip. Had she really said that aloud?

Roy adjusted the kettle to a better position on the flame, then swung around to face her. "What are you talking about? You asked for Nelson, and I told you he was out at the shack."

Kara couldn't hold back a bark of laughter. "He sure wasn't there when I arrived. But someone else was."

His heavy brows drew together over his beaked nose as he extracted a wrapped sandwich and a packet of chips from the paper bag. "I don't know what you're talking about. Nobody here except us chickens." He cracked a crooked smile at his own joke.

"So you say," Kara responded. Roy's attempt at levity didn't succeed in warming her toward the farmhand. She thought about pressing him further, but she decided against it.

She didn't like Roy's shifty, sullen attitude. It was entirely possible he had sent her to the sugar shack on purpose, knowing she would be attacked. Maybe he'd tipped off her assailant—or maybe her assailant had followed her here. However it had happened, now she was alone with Roy in the farmhouse.

She shrank back in her chair, fumbling in her handbag for her phone. In case she needed it.

Though who would possibly reach her in time to save her if Roy attacked?

Sean wasn't exactly dressed for a snowmobile ride, but there was no point in complaining. So he tried to ignore the bone-chilling wind rushing against his face and the snow that sprayed him relentlessly as he and Nelson rode across an open field.

What did a little cold matter in light of a threat to Kara? Sean would never forget his fear when they couldn't find her—and his anger when they did. Break-ins at her aunt's house were bad enough, not to mention a threatening note. But until now, whoever was behind this hadn't touched Kara. Well, besides the incident outside the house.

Sean winced, remembering his own encounter with the intruder. That had been deliberate as well, but he was a police officer, trained to deal with possible violence. Kara was brave, but she was a small, slight woman.

He burned so hotly with rage that the cold spray suddenly felt refreshing against his skin. He couldn't wait to figure out who was behind all this. They needed to find the culprit before things escalated even more. He itched to ramp up the search and put a stop to Kara's torture. His teeth clenched. He wouldn't rest until the person was in jail.

Until then, he had to protect Kara. Even if it meant not letting her out of his sight until this was over. *And maybe never again . . .*

"I found the tracks in the woods!" Nelson shouted over his shoulder as they left the field and shot into a stand of trees. "Just a little farther. How are you doing back there?"

"I'm fine!" Sean shouted back. He braced himself against the sway of the machine as they ascended hills and dipped into hollows. Inside the woods, snow had drifted and the ground wasn't as level as the field. If Nelson miscalculated, they could end up swamped in deep snow or crunched up against a tree.

Sean noticed that Nelson was breaking a new trail with his snowmobile, probably to save time. They passed through the sugar bush, where stands of thick-trunked maples stood waiting for spring, then entered a stand of pines and other evergreens. Sean glimpsed a stone wall in the distance that had been used to mark boundary lines in the distant past.

"Right over here!" Nelson yelled. He slowed the machine, then came to a complete halt.

The sudden silence was almost deafening at first. Then the chirp of a bird and the rush of wind in the treetops filtered in. Nelson climbed off the snowmobile, and Sean followed suit, his legs stiff. His boots sank into powdery snow well above their tops.

"Sorry about that," Nelson said. The farmer was dressed in overalls that protected him from the wet snow.

Sean glanced down at his pants, which were soaked to the knees. "It's fine. I have more important things to worry about." He lumbered forward, eager to see what Nelson had discovered.

Nelson stood by a set of snowmobile tracks. He pointed. "These came from the adjacent fields, which belong to the farm next door." He turned, continuing to point out the route. "Then he cut through there and down to the shack."

Sean bent closer. "And it appears that he came back this way." The imprint in the snow was too deep to have been made by one passage through it.

Nelson adjusted his hat over his ears. "That's what I'm guessing.

I don't understand why someone did this. Was Kara the target, or did she happen to get in the way of something?" He frowned. "But I have no idea what they were doing on my property in the first place. There's nothing of value in the shack. Not even containers of syrup."

Sean knew the answer to Nelson's question. "She's the target all right." He locked eyes with the farmer, wanting to gauge his reaction. "Ever since they found Angela's body, someone has been plaguing her."

Nelson's eyes widened with shock that looked genuine. "Plaguing Kara? But why? What does she have to do with Angela's accident?"

Sean shifted in the snow, another clump of the cold wet stuff sliding into his boot. How much more should he say? He didn't think Nelson was behind the mysterious incidents, but he couldn't be sure he wasn't. He sidestepped the question. "It seems the discovery of Angela's body has set off a chain reaction, and Kara has found herself in the middle of it."

Nelson shook his head. "I don't like the sound of that. And I'm very upset that someone would attack her on my property. Kara was always like a niece to me. In fact, her aunt and I were—"

"Wait," Sean said, putting up a hand. "Kara likely came here today to talk to you about Angela. Why don't we head back? You can tell her yourself."

"All right," Nelson said. He scanned the ground again. "Are you going to take pictures of this? I would. If the temps warm like they say, the tracks will be a blur by tomorrow."

"Good point." Sean extracted his phone from his inner jacket pocket and took photos of the tracks, making sure the camera setting provided enough contrast. Then he took establishing shots. "There's an official trail nearby, isn't there?"

"Yes," Nelson said, indicating the direction. "It follows the river over there."

The snowmobile corridor passing so close to Nelson's property meant that a rider could have accessed the trail at a number of points. Sean would review the area map later and see if anything popped out as a possible clue.

The snow down his boots was melting fast, and Sean knew frozen feet were a bad idea. "I'm ready to go," he said.

"Hop on," Nelson said, throwing his leg over the seat and starting the machine.

The ride back to the farmhouse seemed to take forever. Sean silently urged Nelson on, but the snowmobile was hampered by the snowdrifts and uneven terrain since they didn't return via the same path. They reached the open field at last, and Nelson accelerated, the machine chewing up the distance.

"Here we are," Nelson said as he pulled to a halt near the side entrance. "Want to come in for a warm-up?"

"I sure do," Sean said. His legs were stiff as he climbed off the snowmobile, and his feet felt like solid blocks of ice. "I'll be a minute. I'm going to grab my spare pair of boots and change." He didn't have fresh jeans, so his frozen ones would have to do.

Nelson nodded and went ahead into the house.

Sean hurried to his truck. He thought about changing outside but decided against it. He wanted—no, needed—to see Kara with his own two eyes and make sure she was all right.

Carrying a pair of leather boots and a pair of dry socks, Sean walked right into the house without knocking. The hired hand was eating at the table, Nelson was filling a coffee carafe with water, and Kara sat in the rocking chair with Sadie at her feet.

When Kara glanced at Sean, her face crumpled briefly.

Sean realized that she was scared out of her wits. "What happened while we were gone?" he asked in a deadly tone.

Roy dabbed his mouth with a paper napkin. "What are you talking about?" He shot an aggrieved expression at his boss. "I didn't do anything. Came in to eat my lunch."

"Is that true?" Sean asked Kara.

She nodded.

"Just checking." Sean sent a glare toward Roy that told the man he'd better watch himself, then asked Nelson, "Got a place I can change my socks?"

Nelson gestured toward a doorway next to Sean. "Bathroom right there. Feel free to use one of the towels."

When Sean reentered the kitchen a couple of minutes later, the coffee was perking and Roy was gone. Kara was now at the table, the faithful Sadie still next to her.

"I see you have a new friend," Sean said to lighten the mood, reaching down to pat the retriever's head.

He was rewarded by a smile. "I certainly do," Kara said. "She hasn't left my side the whole time."

Dogs were smart, and Sean wondered if Sadie sensed Kara's emotions. Or maybe the dog sensed that Kara was in danger. From Nelson, now filling three mugs, or that surly hired hand, Roy? Based on his past experience as a cop, Sean didn't trust Roy any farther than he could throw him. He wondered why Nelson kept the man on, although he understood that farm help was hard to come by. Not many people wanted to spend their days cleaning out stalls and taking care of livestock.

Sean pulled out a chair and sat beside Kara. "Someone else was here today," he said. "We found the tracks. They must have cut over from the snowmobile trail."

Kara took this in, her eyes wide. "But how did they know I was at the farm? I didn't tell anyone I was coming here."

"No posts on social media?" Sean cracked a smile to let her know he was joking. But he was continually surprised by how much personal information people put out there for public view. More than one local case had been solved that way.

Nelson carried the mugs over to the table and distributed them, his expression troubled. "I'm very upset this happened to you, Kara. I'll do whatever I can to get to the bottom of it."

Kara looked at the farmer as she tipped cream into her mug. "I'm not blaming you. It's clear that trouble followed me here, and I'm sorry about that."

"I think the trouble started a long time ago," Nelson replied. After delivering that cryptic remark, he wandered over to the counter and picked up a rectangular plastic container, then brought it to the table. He peeled back the lid. "Homemade blueberry muffins. Have one."

Kara took one and nibbled at it. "Are you talking about my aunt? Because I have to agree with you. What was going on with her?" Her voice became pleading. "My mother and I don't know, but she was close to you. Did she tell you anything?"

Nelson sat down. He dispensed sugar into his mug and stirred, obviously thinking. "Not much. Something was going on at work that she wasn't happy about. But when I asked her a week or so later about it, she said everything was fine."

Kara huffed. "So that's a dead end."

"Maybe," Nelson said. "We were enjoying a romantic birthday dinner at her house when I brought it up. I got the feeling then that she didn't want to spoil the mood." His gaze softened, and a small smile lit his face. "It was a memorable evening. I decided that night that I would ask her to marry me."

"Oh!" Kara exclaimed, tears springing to her eyes. "That would have been wonderful." She stood and hobbled over to her handbag. "I found this in her house." She handed a greeting card to Nelson.

While he'd been listening, an idea had blossomed in Sean's mind, and once it lodged in his thoughts, it was like an itch he needed to scratch. With the turn of the conversation, this might be a good time to give them some privacy.

He rose from his seat. "I'll be right back."

Kara and Nelson watched him with mild curiosity, but neither questioned his actions as he hurried over and put on his jacket. They probably thought he needed something from his truck.

Once outside, Sean grabbed a flashlight from his truck, then went over to Kara's car. Using the flashlight, he scanned the data port, between the seats, and under the seats. He felt inside the pockets and opened the glove box. Nothing.

Then he popped the trunk handle and went around. Inside the trunk he discovered a spare tire and a few tools in a plastic case. But then he found a small black box tucked under the rug and magnetically attached.

A GPS tracking device.

19

Sean appeared in the kitchen doorway. "Can you excuse us a moment?" he asked Nelson. "I have something Kara needs to see."

"Take your time," Nelson said. He hadn't stopped staring at the birthday card since Kara had given it to him. Obviously it had triggered a lot of memories.

"What is it?" Kara asked, rising from the table. She couldn't imagine what Sean was referring to, but her heart had begun to pound all the same.

He shook his head, his expression unreadable.

Instead of pressing for an answer, she put on her coat and boots and prepared to go outside.

Sean held the outside door open for her, then followed her across the back porch. "I found something in your car," he murmured.

"What?" Kara jerked to a halt on the steps. "What did you find?"

He put a finger to his lips. "Hang on. I'll show you." He took the lead across the drive to her car.

Kara tagged along on his heels, a thousand questions in her mind.

Sean opened the driver's door and popped the trunk, then signaled for her to join him at the rear of the car. "I think someone followed you here," he said. "But I couldn't figure out how, especially since they arrived on a snowmobile. You said no one knew you were coming to visit Nelson, right?"

"Not even Mom," Kara said. "It's so strange. I didn't even see a single snowmobile on the way. And no one was behind me on the road." She shuddered. "Not like the other day."

A crease appeared between his brows. "What happened the other day?"

Kara waved off his concern. "Something kind of scary but okay in the end. A big black pickup tailgated me and Mom while we were driving out to Everly's Evergreens to get a Christmas tree."

"That's just up the road from here," Sean said. "A black pickup? Did you happen to get the license plate?"

"No, it was covered with mud. The windshield was too, so I couldn't really see the driver." She made a disgusted sound. "Doesn't that figure?"

"Doesn't that figure," Sean echoed in a voice she couldn't read. He began to root around in the trunk. "Anyway, I started to wonder how someone was tracking you. So I took the liberty of searching your car." He gave her a level gaze. "Is that all right with you?"

"It certainly is," Kara said, catching on. "I give you permission to search my car." She felt a smile break across her face. "Even if it is retroactive." Then her stomach sank. "What did you find?"

He peeled back the rug in the corner of the trunk, then stood aside so she could get a good view.

A small black box was attached to the metal frame. She sucked in a breath. "Is that a GPS tracker?" She'd heard of them and thought they were very sneaky devices. What did it say about a person if they wanted to track someone?

"Yes. I've seen them before." Sean seemed to hesitate. "You don't know of anyone who would put a tracker in your car, do you?"

"Like who?" Kara asked, offended. Then she realized what he was asking. "No, I don't have any jealous boyfriends in my life. No boyfriends at all, as a matter of fact."

He didn't respond.

Kara glanced at him. Was that relief she saw in his eyes? When he blinked, she decided she was imagining things. "And I'm old enough that my mother doesn't track my movements. Although if these had been around when I was a teen, she might have used one."

"Sorry, but I had to ask," Sean said. "Since you don't have any idea who could have installed a tracker, with your permission I'm going to remove it and enter it into evidence." His expression was wry. "They can track me until I take the device to the station."

Kara couldn't hold back a laugh. "Maybe they'll follow it there too. Wouldn't that be a hoot?" She sobered. "Yes, you have my permission to remove it. And I hope you find whoever put it in there. What an absolutely rotten thing to do."

"I agree." Sean started to move toward his truck. "Why don't you head back inside? I'll get an evidence bag." He halted. "From now on, lock your car, okay? Everywhere. All the time. Even at home."

"Okay," Kara said. What was this world coming to? Not only were they required to change the locks on the house, but now she had to lock her car in her own driveway. In sweet little Castlebridge.

Sean checked his phone. "We'd better get going. I have to report for duty soon."

"We?" Kara asked, confused.

He squared his shoulders and looked her right in the eye. "I'm going to follow you home to make sure you get there safely."

A chill swept through Kara. "You really think that's necessary?" Even as she said the words, she heard how foolish they sounded. Someone had followed her here and locked her in an empty and cold room. She didn't have anything worse than a few bruises—this time. But what if they tried again while she was on the road?

She swallowed hard, her throat suddenly dry. "That was dumb. You're right. I do need to be careful. Not give whoever it was another chance to attack me."

Sean moved closer. "I'm going to catch that person and arrest them. Enough is enough."

Kara stared at him, and to her horror, she felt tears flood her eyes. "Who's behind this? And why? I don't know anything. I was a kid when Aunt Angela disappeared."

He regarded her, his expression tight and intense.

For a moment, she had the feeling he was going to sweep her into his arms. Her skin tingled, and she swayed forward, longing to shelter again in the safety he offered.

Her pulse leaped. *Something is happening. Maybe already has.* Kara had thought she was totally over Sean, that all the flames were out, like campfire coals doused with cold water. She'd been angry with him for so long. And after that, she'd felt merely indifferent, their relationship a bittersweet memory from the distant past.

Sean stepped back, the space between them cooling as a gust of wind swirled across the farmyard.

Sharp disappointment stabbed her, and she turned away, using her bare hand to swipe at the tears threatening to freeze on her cheeks.

"We'd better get going," he said again, his voice strangely hoarse. "I'm not making any progress standing here, freezing my toes off."

His comment made Kara laugh, loosening the tightness in her chest. "My fingers are already blocks of ice." She thrust them into her jacket pockets.

Inside the farmhouse, Nelson was still seated at the table, the birthday card next to his mug. "Ready for a warm-up?" he asked.

"Actually, we need to get going," Kara said. "But thank you."

Nelson stood up with a grunt. "Thank me for what? I'm sorry—" He broke off.

Kara didn't respond. She knew what he was going to say.

"Hang on a minute." Nelson went to a door across the kitchen and opened it, revealing a walk-in pantry. He pulled a string to switch on the light, then disappeared inside. He returned with two jugs of maple syrup. "Here you go. Merry Christmas."

Kara took the jug he offered, cradling it in the crook of her arm. "Thank you. Mom is going to be so happy."

"And so is Miss Eleanor," Sean said, lifting the jug. "I'll split this with her. There's plenty."

For a moment, Kara was disconcerted at the mention of Miss Eleanor, but then she remembered. She was Sean's landlady and well over eighty years old.

"Thanks for bringing that card." Nelson pulled the pantry light switch. "It brought back so many good memories. Do you know the Castle River covered bridge?"

"Of course." Kara remembered the embroidery her aunt had made.

"That was where your aunt and I went on our first date." Nelson smiled at the memory. "On our way back from dinner, we parked there and walked out onto the bridge. She challenged me to a stick race."

"That's so cute." Kara had played stick race with her aunt numerous times. Each person tossed a small stick over the side of the bridge and then raced to the other side to see whose emerged first. Now it made sense why Angela had left the embroidery to Nelson—as a memento of their first date. But she hadn't expected to die, so why add that to the will? If they'd gotten married, as Nelson believed, he would own it anyway.

Puzzled, Kara decided not to mention the bequest to Nelson yet. She wanted to examine the work carefully before it left her possession. Another idea struck. She could find out when the will had been updated to include the picture. She could be way out on a limb, but it was something to investigate.

And right now she was fresh out of other ideas.

As promised, Sean followed her home, his large truck looming in her rearview mirror. But this time Kara didn't feel threatened or uneasy. She felt calm and safe. Once again Sean had come to her rescue. And while she didn't like to think of herself as a damsel in distress—she could take care of herself, thank you—she had to admit it was nice.

As they drove through the countryside toward Castlebridge, Kara thought back to the days of their relationship. They'd started out as lab partners in a chemistry class. Soon they'd discovered that they shared the same wacky sense of humor, and they'd bonded over the absurdities of their teacher. Mr. Morris had been comical, wearing glasses on a chain and making frequent wry comments about his students' lack of diligence. Unfortunately he'd also become quite absentminded. He hadn't noticed when another pair of students almost added the wrong item to a solution. Sean called out in the nick of time to prevent an explosion. The beloved Mr. Morris had retired soon after, ending his fifty-year run.

Sean saved the day then, and he's still busy saving it now. When he'd confided to Kara that he wanted to become a police officer, she hadn't been surprised. After all, his uncle was the chief, and Sean's logical mind and protective nature were a natural fit for the profession.

They finally arrived at her mother's, and Sean insisted on going inside and checking out the house while Kara waited in the car. He returned a few minutes later, and she got out of the car.

"The house is empty," Sean said. "I walked the perimeter of Angela's house too, and all the doors and windows are intact." He pressed the keys into her hand, holding it for a long moment.

Kara met his eyes, and she found herself unable to look away.

"I'll be in touch," he said. "If anything at all happens, you call my cell. Promise?"

"I promise." She glanced at the house with its snow-covered roof, sitting peacefully in the afternoon sun. "I'll lock the doors. I don't have any plans for the rest of the day. Just hanging out and listening to Christmas music. Making dinner for Mom."

Sean nodded. "Sounds nice."

Was she imagining the wistful note in his voice? She *knew* she wasn't imagining the disappointment she felt as he walked to his truck and pulled away from the curb.

Kara grabbed her handbag and the jug of syrup from the car. She started toward the house, then paused and clicked the fob, hoping her neighbor didn't notice. It felt foolish.

Yes, she locked her car downtown and in parking lots. But here in this quiet neighborhood, she'd never done that before today. When she reminded herself that someone had taken advantage of that and put a tracking device in her car, she suddenly didn't feel foolish anymore.

Her gaze fell on the mailbox. She really should check the mail, instead of leaving it for her mother.

The black metal box was stuffed full with flyers, bills, and Christmas card envelopes. And she'd seen a stack of cards in the house already. In years past, they'd taped them up around the living room doorway, a colorful display of Christmas cheer. That was something she could do today. Then she could check out Castlebridge Christmas Days downtown and buy some presents. She still hadn't gotten her mother anything yet, and cashmere sweaters were on sale in one of the boutiques.

She balanced the load in her arms and went inside. The house was warm and cozy, and after locking up and kicking off her boots, she headed directly for the kitchen and dumped everything on the table. She hung her coat on the back of a kitchen chair, then put on the kettle for hot chocolate. A metal tin sat on the counter, and she opened it to reveal an assortment of Christmas cookies. She chose a frosted reindeer sugar cookie and took a bite. The library staff did a cookie exchange every year, and this must be the result.

While waiting for the kettle to boil, Kara located the opened cards and added the new ones to the pile. She grabbed the tape dispenser out of the junk drawer. After making a mug of cocoa, she went into the living room to work.

Before starting, she loaded the woodstove and lit the fire, then plugged in the Christmas tree. The lights made the assorted ornaments glitter, and Kara paused to touch a few of her favorites. In addition to colored balls, her mother had collected quaint decorations featuring New England as well as homemade ones crafted by Kara through the years. Decorating the tree was like taking a trip through time.

The last step was turning on seasonal music, and then Kara sat on the ottoman to open the new cards. She recognized many of the names—distant relatives, neighbors, and family friends. There was a pretty card from Miss Eleanor, Sean's landlady. Kara smiled, remembering how she'd been a little unsettled earlier until she realized who he was talking about.

She stopped ripping open another envelope to think. Did she still have feelings for Sean? Or were they only fleeting remnants of what once was?

Her cheeks heated as she recalled the scene at the farm. She had almost thrown herself into his arms. What had she been thinking? What if he'd pushed her away? For all she knew, he could be serious about another woman.

And here she was, ready to fall at his feet. Mortified, Kara ripped the envelope seal with a little more vigor than was needed.

A card depicting a cute snowman was inside. Smiling, she opened the card to read the message.

I told you to stay out of it. Don't you listen?

Sean drove slowly away from Kara's house, peering into the rearview mirror for a final glimpse of her. He hated to leave, but he had no choice. Not unless he called in and took a leave day. He laughed at his own foolishness. And then what would he do? He didn't think she'd take kindly to being babysat.

He barely had time to go home and change, but by some miracle, he was dressed and ready within ten minutes. One thing he definitely had to do today was check the vehicle log again. Last night there hadn't been an entry for the other cruiser. But sometimes people were slack about filling out the log, especially at night.

Sean also had the tracker from Kara's car to enter into evidence. He'd been careful handling it in case there were fingerprints, but he really didn't hold out hope that it would be that easy. Maybe once he filed a report about the attack on Kara and the tracking device on her car, the chief would have to listen to him. Something rotten was going on, and they needed to get to the bottom of it.

Before someone else was seriously injured—or worse.

Sean frowned. Why did the idea of pushing the issue with the chief make his stomach knot up? Was it because his uncle had been his mentor? Who was he to challenge the man who had taught him everything?

But things weren't adding up in the department either. Sean didn't like the way the chief had brushed off his concerns and implied that Kara was in league with the intruder. The intruder who had punched

Sean last night. He doubted it was a second prowler. *Wait until the other officers see my black eye.* Assaulting an officer was hard to ignore.

Eager to get started, Sean quickly refreshed Bandit's food and water bowls, then ran down the stairs and emerged from the garage.

Miss Eleanor popped her head out the back door. "Can I talk to you for a minute?" Her voice was tremulous.

Inwardly he groaned, knowing that lingering to speak to her might make him late. But if something was wrong with his dear landlady and friend and he ignored her, he would never forgive himself.

"Sure thing," he said, changing direction back toward the porch.

"I won't keep you," she said. "I can see you're on the way to work."

Sean was relieved that she looked fine. Uninjured, healthy, fully dressed, and with her hair neatly combed. "No problem," he said. "I'm here for you anytime."

Miss Eleanor tapped a finger against her lips. "Ever since we had that chat earlier, I've been thinking. And I remembered something. Miles wasn't the only person to visit George. Angela came over here a few weeks before her disappearance."

Sometimes while working a case, Sean had come across information that felt like finding a missing puzzle piece that he'd been searching for all along, but he hadn't quite been sure of the color or shape. He was certain that Angela's visit to George meant something. But like a picture slowly emerging from a heap of images, he wasn't quite sure *what* exactly.

"Before you ask, I have no idea what they discussed," she added. "It was in his study, and the door was shut."

"Thanks," he said, bending to kiss her soft cheek. "If you remember anything else related to Miles or Angela, call me, okay?"

Her eyes gleamed with satisfaction. "I'm glad to do anything I can to help that sweet young woman and her mother." She raised an eyebrow at him. "And I'm guessing you feel the same way. Didn't you and Kara used to date?"

With a groan, Sean tried to laugh it off. "Yeah, ages ago. Back in high school. I'm just doing my job, that's all."

As he made his way down the steps, he distinctly heard Miss Eleanor say in a low voice, "Keep telling yourself that. You can't fool me." The kitchen door shut with a decisive *click*.

Sean chuckled to himself. He loved Miss Eleanor to pieces, even her habit of putting her finger right on the pain point. His investigation into Angela's death had gone far beyond his duty. He had to admit he'd continue even if he wasn't paid—for Kara.

Despite driving as fast as was legal, Sean arrived at the station a few minutes late.

Ryan was at the front desk reading a newspaper, and he glanced up with a smirk. "Glad you could make it. The chief made me wait until you got here so I could clock out." Then his eyes widened. "What happened to you?"

Sean didn't bother to reply. He was hardly ever late and often worked overtime. He was halfway to his desk when he remembered. Striding back to the front desk, he asked, "Did you sign out a cruiser while I was on shift last night?" He gave the time.

The other officer frowned and went back to the paper. "No. I was Christmas shopping with Bethany at the mall." Bethany was his girlfriend.

The fact that Sean had seen the police car well after the mall shops closed wasn't lost on him. But rather than pursue the issue now, he nodded and kept going. After hanging up his jacket, he set his phone and the GPS tracker on his desk and prepared to file his reports.

"Sean?" the chief called out from his office. "Is that you? I need to talk to you."

A snicker floated back from the front desk. That was why Ryan was lingering instead of rushing to clock out. He'd known that the chief wanted to speak to Sean and was hoping to see his fellow officer get in trouble.

"What is it?" Sean asked, stopping in the chief's doorway. Maybe it would be quick.

But then his superior gestured for him to take a seat.

Once Sean was settled in his chair, the chief, who had been rocking in his own seat, said, "I had an interesting call a little while ago."

"Is that so?" Sean asked, racking his brain. What could the chief possibly be talking about? He released a breath. Maybe he was going to give him a new assignment.

The chief stopped rocking and fixed him with a glare. "Nelson Reed called. That name ring a bell?"

Nelson had called? But Sean had been under the impression that what happened at the farm was his own case. Why had the farmer involved the chief?

The chief swiveled around and clasped his hands on the desk. "Apparently an intruder assaulted Kara Foxworth at the farm this morning. Nelson was very upset about it."

Sean's core went cold. He'd planned to broach the subject after he'd had a chance to get his thoughts in order. But he had to come clean about his involvement now. "I can vouch for that. I was there."

"So I understand," the chief said. "This isn't about how you handled the situation. I understand from Nelson that you helped him figure out how the perp got to the farm."

Relief whooshed through Sean. He wasn't in trouble after all. *Not this time, Ryan.* "Yeah, we took a ride out into the woods and found fresh snowmobile tracks accessing the land." He patted his pocket, then remembered his phone was on his desk. "I took pictures."

"Good, good." The chief eyed him. "What else?"

"I found a tracker in Kara's trunk," Sean answered. "It's on my desk in an evidence bag. That's how the assailant knew she was at the farm. She had gone out to see Nelson and talk about her aunt because they used to be an item."

"A tracker, huh?" The chief rubbed his chin. "Maybe it's a disgruntled boyfriend?"

Denials rushed to Sean's lips, but he let them die. This wasn't a good time for floating hasty theories.

His uncle nodded. "So we know why Kara was there." He paused—a heavy, laden silence. "How about you? Why were you there?"

"I went—" Sean broke off. His claim that he'd gone out to the farm to buy maple syrup sounded incredibly weak. "The truth is, I went out to talk to Nelson." He bowed his head, waiting for the disciplinary action he was sure would follow. "Besides Kara and her mother, he was the most important person in Angela Foxworth's life."

The chief was silent for a long moment. "That was enterprising of you," he finally said. "But I fail to see why it was necessary. Angela's death was an accident."

No, it wasn't. Not wanting to commit career suicide—any more than he already had—Sean kept that thought to himself. He couldn't afford to annoy his uncle and risk not getting a good recommendation. Only a little longer and he would be done with Castlebridge and on his way to joining the state police.

"Perhaps you're right," Sean said. "When you look at it that way, I'm not sure why I was there." He cringed at his own words. Why didn't he come clean, tell him all his thoughts and suspicions? Everything he'd learned? He really didn't know, but something deep inside was warning him not to.

The chief stared at him a little longer before nodding. "In the end, it's a good thing you were there. Nelson certainly praised you to high heaven." He rocked back in his chair. "Get to work."

Sean jumped up, relieved. He'd been expecting a serious reprimand, even to be suspended. "Will do. Thanks."

"And keep me apprised of your movements, will you?" Chief Colton called after him. "I don't want to learn about them from a citizen again."

Sean turned in the doorway. "Fair enough." He'd have to be more careful. He wasn't going to step back until he knew that Kara was safe. And he had the feeling that meant getting to the bottom of her aunt's so-called accident.

Maybe her father's death deserved another pass as well. With new resolve, Sean rushed to his desk.

He soon discovered that the digital records of Miles Foxworth's accident were sketchy, including the bare minimum, with a ruling that the incident had been an accident. He had gone off the road on Dead Man's Curve and hit a large pine tree. Sean winced. Death had been instantaneous—a small comfort. As with Angela's accident, roads had been clear if not totally dry, but black ice had been considered a possible factor.

Sean sat back in his chair. Hard copies were still stored in the records room, so it might be worth checking. Acting more out of instinct than certainty, Sean made his way there. He was supposed to go out on patrol soon, but if he hurried he could at least locate the file.

Thanks to Rhonda's neat filing skills, he quickly found the accident report, a manila folder stuffed with paperwork. A quick flip through revealed more forms and notes than were in the digital file, which was odd.

Sean made a note of where he'd found the file and carried it to his desk. A glance at the clock told him he had exactly five minutes before he needed to head out.

There was nothing new in the paperwork, but he noticed something as he scanned the photographs from the scene. There were skid marks on the tar in the northbound lane, the one Miles had been traveling.

But there was another set of tire tracks in the picture. They were in the same northbound lane. But they started in the southbound lane, as if someone had been coming down the hill and crossed the center line.

The truth hit Sean like a blow to his solar plexus. It was entirely possible that another car had been involved in Miles's accident. The cause of it, as a matter of fact.

So why was there no mention of the other vehicle in the report?

Kara's hand shook as she stared at the Christmas card. *There's some holiday cheer.* With a snort of anger, she tossed the card. It fluttered through the air and landed on the carpet a short distance away.

For a moment, she was tempted to burn it in the stove, watch with glee as the paper caught fire and crumpled into black ash.

But then common sense reigned. The card was evidence, like the note, that someone was threatening her. And she still didn't know why.

After retrieving the card, she photographed it and added the pictures to a text message addressed to Sean. At some point she'd need to take it to the station or have him pick it up, but she thought it was best to inform him right away.

Before sending the text, she remembered the envelope. She really ought to send a picture of that as well, since it might hold clues. She dug through the heap of discarded envelopes next to the ottoman. All of them had stamps and postmarks except one. Knowing the truth immediately, she matched up the snowman card with the envelope. A perfect fit.

Someone had delivered the card to the mailbox in person, obviously not caring that doing so was a federal crime. Well, what was that misdeed in light of sending her threats? Not really a consideration, she guessed.

Her cell phone rang, Neil's name flashing onto the screen. Should she answer? At first she was tempted to let it go to voice mail. But that was the coward's way.

Kara answered, keeping her tone cool. She decided it was better not to let him think she was eager to hear from him, which she wasn't.

"Hey." His voice was warm and friendly. "How are you doing?"

"I'm fine," she said. "Sitting by the fire and opening Christmas cards." Her gaze fell on the snowman. *And threats.*

He laughed. "Sounds like the perfect thing to do on a winter afternoon." A beat. "The reason I'm calling is, I wanted to invite you to a tour."

Kara pulled back and stared at the phone. *A tour of what?* "Um, really?"

The tempo of his voice picked up. "Yeah, we've been doing tons of work at the old mill. I'm sure you've heard about it. Part of it houses businesses, but one building is going to be apartments. Anyway, we're going to have an open house tonight for a small group of selected guests only. A sneak preview."

"I don't know." How could she get out of this? "I'm going Christmas shopping, and then I'm having dinner with my mom."

"It will be after dinner. Just an hour or so." Again the brief hesitation. This time what Neil said floored her. "I thought you might want to see the place, especially since your dad designed a lot of it."

"My dad? But he . . ." Her voice trailed off. Her dad had died more than ten years ago. How was this possible?

"I know." His tone grew somber, almost reverential. "These projects can take a long time to come to fruition. Your father's firm was involved in the initial stages. When we dusted off the plans, we decided to incorporate them. He was ahead of his time. Absolutely brilliant."

This praise was like water on Kara's parched heart. She loved hearing that people had respected her father's work and that he had been regarded as a talented architect.

"Thank you. I'm so happy to hear this." She paused. "Can my mother come along?" She would definitely want to see a project designed by her husband.

"No, I'm afraid not." Neil sounded regretful. "It's a very small group. I had to twist Dad's arm to let me invite a guest."

Her mother would be disappointed, but maybe Kara could take photos. "All right. I'll be there. Tell me where and when."

Dinner was almost on the table when her mother walked in a few minutes after six. "Something smells good," she said, hanging up her coat. "I'm starving."

Kara came to greet her mother with a kiss. "That's because you made the sauce," she said. "Did you forget?"

Her mom smoothed her hair, which had been mussed by a hat. "No, but I thought I smelled garlic bread."

"You did," Kara said. She took her mother's arm and guided her to the living room doorway. "Look what I did this afternoon."

The snowman card and its envelope were safely stowed away in a plastic resealable bag, ready to be delivered to the police. She had resolved not to show her mother the card or discuss what had happened at the farm. What would be the point of upsetting her? Sean was on the case, and that knowledge gave Kara comfort.

Her mother took in the display of colorful Christmas cards. "I love it. Thanks for putting them up." She went to the closest card, which contained a lovely winter scene, and read the inside. "From one of my oldest friends. I'm so glad we still exchange cards."

Kara's gaze flicked over the cards, admiring their variety. "It is really fun." She pointed to the tree. "And no peeking under there," she said with a grin.

Her mom did anyway, exclaiming over the wrapped presents. Buying gifts for each other and putting them out early was another holiday ritual. "Castlebridge Christmas Days?" she guessed.

Kara nodded.

"My turn to go tomorrow."

A timer went off in the kitchen. "That's my cue," Kara said. "I've got to drain the pasta."

In the kitchen, Kara bustled about, putting the finishing touches on the meal. She urged her mother to sit down and not lift a finger. "You've done this for me about a million times," she said against her mom's protests. "So relax."

Soon they were saying grace before tucking into spaghetti with meatballs, a Caesar salad, and thick slices of garlic bread.

They ate quietly for a few minutes before Kara said, "I'm going out for a while tonight, if that's okay with you."

Her mother gave her a puzzled look. "Sure. I plan to curl up by the fire with a good book. Where are you going, if I might ask?"

"No secret," Kara said. "Neil Fuller invited me to take a tour of his new mill project. A small group is going." She'd decided not to mention that her dad had participated in the design. It would hurt her mom's feelings to be excluded from that.

Her mother raised her eyebrows. "Another date with Neil. Huh." There was a world of opinion in that single exclamation, which was not like her mother. She never pried into Kara's private life, and she shared her thoughts about people and situations only when pressed. As she'd said more than once, Kara was an adult, and she trusted her daughter to make the right choices.

Kara's face heated. "Don't worry. I'm not considering it a date. I wasn't even going to see him again. But he sounded so eager to show off his new project, and I didn't have the heart to say no."

Her mom set her fork down. "That's where it starts. I'm sorry, but I don't trust Neil in the least. Don't forget that I saw him in action plenty of times in high school." She had been a parent volunteer, helping with bake sales and sporting events and serving as chaperone at dances and on field trips.

"People change," Kara said, but her words were feeble. She knew Neil hadn't changed. Why should he? He'd been on top of the world all his life.

Her mother picked up her fork again and began to twist it into the heap of spaghetti on her plate. "It's not that I resent him for always being the most popular, the one most likely to succeed. Or that he's the son of the wealthiest man in town."

"I know," Kara said. "You're not like that." Although plenty of people were envious and disliked the Fullers for exactly those reasons.

"No," her mom continued, as if Kara hadn't spoken. "He's a bully, and bullies never change. I tried to step in a couple of times, but even the principal was under Benedict Fuller's thumb. My complaints went nowhere."

Kara regarded her mother with alarm. Apparently she'd been so lost in her own world that she hadn't noticed the bullying. "I didn't know anything about that. What did he do?"

"It's not important now. It had to do with Neil and the other boys. You weren't there."

"That's terrible," Kara said. At her job, she'd seen children bullying each other. In her particular school, these situations were handled swiftly. But she knew that wasn't the case in many places. Probably because some adults sympathized with bullies. Or they were too weak to stand up to them, afraid of the fallout from the parents. Like the high school principal here in Castlebridge.

"It is," her mom agreed. "Especially since Neil had everything and the children he attacked . . . did not."

"'For everyone to whom much is given, from him much will be required,'" Kara quoted. Her father had drilled that particular Bible verse into her head.

Her mother smiled. "You remember that, do you? Your father was so adamant about your Sunday school attendance."

"He taught me that one himself," Kara said. "And another one. 'The apple doesn't fall from the tree.'"

"That's not in the Bible." Her mom was now using the fork to gather another mouthful of pasta.

"I know," Kara said. "I was thinking of Neil's father. Hasn't he been trying to bully everyone in this neighborhood?"

Her mom chewed and swallowed. "You are so right. He couches it in polite terms, but that's exactly what he's doing. Thanks for mentioning it. I'll make that point at our next neighborhood meeting."

Kara dug into her salad. "Glad I could be of help. So anyway, I'll be gone a little while tonight. Oh, the locksmith came and installed security cameras and new locks next door. Be sure to lock your car and the house, in case the prowler returns."

She'd tried to sound unconcerned, but her mother reacted with alarm anyway. "Do you really think he might?"

"Probably not," Kara said. "Who's that stupid? Also, Sean promised to patrol here more often."

Her mom's gaze was shrewd. "And what's going on there?"

What was going on? Once again Kara thought of that heady moment at the farm when she'd almost collapsed into Sean's arms.

She still wasn't certain if the emotion had been one-sided. And if it hadn't been, if Sean still cared for her, could she ever trust him again?

That ship has already sailed, a little voice said. *I do trust him—and those old feelings are far from dead.*

Aware that her mother was staring at her, Kara shook herself. Had she just admitted to herself that she still loved Sean? Wow. She hadn't seen that coming.

"I guess time will tell," Kara finally said, trying to laugh.

Her mom nodded, but her expression was knowing. "Uh-huh." She dabbed her mouth with a napkin and changed the subject. "Can you please pass me the garlic bread?"

Kara set off from the house around seven, which gave her plenty of time to get to the mill, located in the heart of downtown. She'd been in a daze the rest of dinner, stunned by her realization about Sean. That had swiftly been followed by a gnawing anxiety about his feelings for her. The last thing she wanted to do was make a fool of herself over Sean Colton. Once in a lifetime was enough.

Thinking back over his words and actions the last couple of days, Kara had to admit he'd been more than considerate. He'd been worried about her—and her mother—and he'd gone out of his way to help them and be there when he was needed.

He'd even gotten a black eye for his troubles. Kara smiled at the memory of his arrival at her door early that morning. And after that, he'd come to her rescue at the farm. She could still feel her sheer relief when he had burst through that door.

Perhaps she was suffering from a little hero worship. Anyone would under these circumstances. Probably in a week or so, her feelings would change again.

Relieved by this conclusion, Kara squared her shoulders. She'd go to the tour and leave as soon as possible. Maybe she'd been confused about Sean, but she was certain when it came to Neil. She was not interested in him at all.

Metal clanged as Kara drove over the bridge leading to the mill. The first three-story brick building housed businesses, so it was dark at this time of evening. Neil had told her to keep going around the back and enter the wing that would become apartments.

It really was wonderful that they had been able to repurpose these buildings. In some towns, old mills sat crumbling, a constant reminder of a more prosperous past.

The parking lot was pretty dark, barely lit by the scattered sodium lights. The asphalt here was rough, a minefield of potholes. Obviously they hadn't gotten around to resurfacing yet.

Neil's car and a couple of pickups were in the lot. *Hmm. I must be early.*

Kara parked as close as she could to the well-lit entrance. After locking the car, she headed inside through a glass-paneled door.

The space was obviously under construction. The square entrance hall she'd entered had drywall on the walls but hadn't been painted yet. Ladders, tools, tarps, and sealed five-gallon buckets filled one corner.

Several doors led off the entrance, one to each side and a double set straight ahead.

Kara hesitated, not sure which way to go. She pulled out her phone to call Neil for directions. Her message app opened, and she saw that she hadn't sent Sean the pictures of the snowman card. For a moment, she wondered why, then remembered she'd been interrupted by Neil's call. She sent the text to Sean and scrolled through for Neil's message so she could call him.

A man pushed through the double doors. He was somehow familiar with his stocky frame. He grinned when he saw Kara. "Here to see Neil?"

"Yes, I'm here for the tour." She laughed. "I think I'm early."

The man gestured for her to follow. "Come this way." He held one side of the double doors open for her.

As they set off along a corridor, this one freshly painted and with new tile floors, Kara asked, "Do I know you from somewhere?"

The man shrugged. "Maybe. People tell me I have that kind of face."

The hallway seemed endless, the only sound the squeaking of their shoes on the shiny tiles. Doors on each side were firmly shut, with no indication of what was behind them. She wondered if they were part of the student housing.

"Where is he?" Kara asked. "This place is huge."

"It's pretty big. He's right up here."

They reached another set of double doors, and her companion pushed through one of them, holding it open with his bulk.

The room was cavernous and dimly lit. Kara guessed it was some kind of dining hall or community room.

Neil was at the far end, sitting at a big table with a few tools and some blueprints scattered over the surface. Hanging lamps made his blond hair glow. He slid off a stool. "Glad you could make it."

Kara crossed the room, taking it in. Tall windows lined the wall on the river side, and quirky metal chandeliers hung from a post-and-beam ceiling. Even unfurnished, she could tell the design was a nice mix of traditional and modern. Was this her father's work?

"Where is everyone?" she asked Neil. "Did the tour get canceled?" Her voice echoed in the empty room. Unease made her skin prickle. Had he lied to get her here alone? But why? Nothing made sense.

Neil patted the stool beside him. "Sit. I want to talk to you."

He hadn't answered the question. A cold wave of fear drenched her. What was going on? She turned, ready to leave, not caring what Neil wanted. She needed to get out of here.

Roy, the handyman from the farm, slipped through the door. Kara stared in shock. The farmhand and the other man took positions in front of the double doors, their posture signaling that they would prevent her from leaving.

She was trapped.

"Aren't you going out on patrol?" the chief asked Sean. He stood in the doorway of his office. Lines furrowed his forehead. "What are you working on?"

"Nothing important," Sean said, flipping the file closed. "Sorry about that. I guess the time got away from me." He slid the file into the drawer of his desk that locked, and shut it firmly. "I'm going out now."

"You do that," the chief said. He disappeared back into his office.

For the next few hours, Sean patrolled Castlebridge, driving up and down Main Street, through the neighborhoods, and out to the town limits. It was a quiet night overall. He stopped one person for speeding and gave her a warning. At a gas station, he helped another unlock his car after leaving the keys inside.

It was a typical quiet shift in Castlebridge, and tonight he was grateful for it. Operating almost automatically gave him time to think about Miles Foxworth. Had he been deliberately driven off the road? Or had the accident been just that—an accident, another casualty of Dead Man's Curve? Drivers tended to come down the hill too fast, often crossing the line into the other lane. From the location of the skid marks, that could have happened.

Why hadn't the chief investigated it? That question nagged at Sean. The report plainly said there had been no witnesses, so no one had come forward. If it had happened now, Sean would have made it his business to search high and low for the other driver.

Deciding to swing by Kara's house, he called in and signed off for his dinner break. The protocol was that he kept his radio on, of course, in case something happened and they needed him.

Michelle answered his knock. "Why, hello. How are you?"

He put his fingers to his hat brim. "I'm fine. Thanks. And you?"

"We're great." Michelle studied him, a smile in her eyes. "I didn't call 911, so I'm guessing you're here to see Kara."

Sean nodded. "Is she available?"

"I'm sorry, but she's not in at the moment. She went to the old mill for some kind of tour."

"The old mill?" Sean repeated. He had been by there more than once tonight, and the place had seemed deserted.

"Yes, the Fuller Mill. I guess they're doing some work inside, and Neil wanted Kara to check it out."

Neil, huh? First dinner, and now an after-hours tour. Sean pushed aside his jealousy and thought about that. A building under construction wouldn't be his choice for a second date. But Neil did have a huge ego, and maybe he thought showing off his work and wealth would impress Kara. Which proved how little he knew her.

His cell phone bleeped with a message. "Excuse me," he said, pulling it out. "I'd better check this."

The message was from Kara, and it contained pictures of a Christmas card, front and envelope, then inside. He used his fingers to enlarge the picture and read the handwritten note scrawled under the printed greeting.

His blood went cold. Another threat. At a glance, the handwriting was similar to the note at the college.

He tucked away the phone. "I'm sorry, but I've got to go."

Maybe he was overreacting, but he'd feel better once he tracked Kara down and made sure she was okay.

23

"What is this?" Kara asked Neil. She rummaged in her handbag for her phone. If she didn't get a good answer, she was going to call for help.

"I just want to talk to you," Neil said, his tone wheedling. "About your father."

Kara's head jerked up. Maybe she was reading too much into this whole situation. "About Dad? His designs?" She withdrew her hand from her bag.

Neil tapped one of the blueprints on the table, held down at the corners with mugs and a tape measure. "Yeah, take a look. This wing used to be a big, open production floor. But he figured out how to reconfigure the space to make rooms, a dining hall, and smaller community rooms."

Kara studied the blueprint, barely understanding the lines and legend. "That sounds good," she said. "Why didn't your company build it before?"

"Why do you think?" Neil asked. "Money, obviously. It took a while to get that lined up. We also had to stabilize the building and clean it up from the manufacturing process." His voice cracked. "And to be honest, losing your dad from the project was a real setback."

Surprised by this admission, Kara stared at Neil—and froze when she saw the small gun in his hand. "What are you doing?" Her voice was sure and strong, even though that was far from how she felt.

He held out his other hand, a wry smile on his face. "Give me your phone." When she hesitated, he waved the gun. "Now."

She scrabbled inside her handbag. "Why? What's going on?" Panic made her heart race. Her fingers trembled as she extracted the phone, her lifeline to help. She dropped it onto the table, heart sinking.

Neil put the phone into his pants pocket. "Sit," he said again, and this time it was a command.

Kara perched on the edge of a stool. "Don't do this. I'm no threat to you." Light dawned. "Did you kill my aunt? Is that what this is all about?"

His eyes widened, then narrowed. "You know what it's about. The research you were doing at the college library."

"About Dad?" Kara felt her mouth drop open with understanding. "You were involved in his accident?" The police had told her and her mother that it was a single-car accident. Her dad had gone off the road and hit a tree. End of story.

Neil shook his head, wincing as if in pain. "I was there, okay? Tiffany broke up with me, and I was upset. Drank too much. Was speeding. My car crossed the line. Your dad swerved to avoid me."

The mental pictures Kara had of her dad's accident underwent revision. She pictured his panic when headlights appeared and headed right toward him, forcing him off the road. "But why weren't you arrested for drunk driving? Why weren't we told the truth?"

His eyes were sad. "It was obviously covered up. Otherwise, the rest of my life would have been ruined. My college acceptances pulled. I'd have to go through a trial. I'd have a record. Vehicular manslaughter. Maybe even jail time."

"How did you get away with it?" Kara asked. Her whole body shook with anger. "Did you drive off and leave him there?"

"No," Neil said, seeming offended by this question. "I called for help. But since I never actually hit him, they were able to write it up as a single-car accident. My father, Chief Colton, and Walter Hill were involved. Don't you know anything? We Fullers own this town."

The chief was complicit? Did that mean Sean was too?

No. Kara refused to believe that he would do anything like that.

"I'm starting to get the picture," Kara said. "But still, why are you doing this? I'm not a threat to you." Well, she hadn't been until his confession. Once she got out of here—and she had to believe that she would get out—she was going straight to the police. The state police.

Neil shook his head. "There's more. Your aunt was going to bring everything down. Why didn't she mind her own business?" He leveled a sad expression at her. "Why didn't *you*?"

Kara's pulse spiked. So she had been right. Aunt Angela had come across something in the course of her work.

"We have an . . . arrangement with the college." Neil waved the gun, gesturing at the big room. "None of this is cheap. But fortunately Everett was able to help us stay afloat. He has some hefty endowments. He's been a silent partner."

Although far from a financial expert, Kara could put two and two together. The college president had illicitly used college funds to help keep the Fuller companies afloat. And Angela must have figured it out.

Kara put a hand to her mouth, feeling sick to her stomach as the truth dawned. "You murdered my aunt."

"I didn't do it personally," Neil said. "But yes, you're right. Her so-called accident wasn't one. It was totally staged."

"Who killed her?" Kara demanded.

Neil motioned toward the doorway where the sentinels still stood. "You can thank Roy for that. He caught up with her while she was on her way to the attorney general's office to report Dad and the others. After that, we started the rumor that she'd run off with another man. Since her boss was the source, everyone believed it."

"That's not fair," Roy protested. "I was only doing what I was told. Your old man came up with the plan. He told me and Ernie to hit her on the head and then dispose of her car—with her inside." He gave a dry chuckle. "We sure did a good job, didn't we? Took ten years for someone to find it."

Kara froze, scarcely able to process this new revelation. It was one thing to suspect foul play and quite another to hear blunt confirmation of it. And *Ernie*—where had she heard that name? She suddenly realized he was the maintenance man at the college. That was why he seemed familiar. He must have switched off the lights and left the threatening note for her.

"You were paid handsomely for it," Neil snapped. "And for spying on Angela and Nelson. Good thing for him that he doesn't know anything." He made a slicing motion across his throat. "Or else."

More pieces clicked into place. Roy's job at the farm had allowed him to keep an eye on Nelson, first with Angela and then alone. And Ernie worked at the college, along with her mother. Both were part of Benedict Fuller's network.

One thing still confused her. "So why did you break into Angela's house?" Kara asked. "Hadn't you already confiscated any proof my aunt had of your crimes?"

"Not my crimes," Neil corrected. "But yes. When she was found, Dad wanted to be sure that we did have everything. So we took another look in her car and then at the house. Roy was handling that department and basically failed." He glared at Roy. "Isn't that right?"

"I would have finished the job sooner or later," Roy growled. "I'm still gonna try." He jerked his chin toward Kara. "Now that you're getting her out of the way. Why didn't you keep your nose out of it, lady?"

Kara was beginning to wonder the same thing. She'd had no idea what a can of worms she'd opened. And no one else did either. The Fullers had created an almost impenetrable aura of success and wealth. Who would ever suspect them of these crimes?

Sean would. Where was he? He'd shown up to help her so many times already, as if they had some kind of invisible connection. Would tonight be the one time he didn't come? The time when she needed him most?

As if reading her mind, Roy spoke up. "That cop who's been following you around has got to go."

"I guess he doesn't understand who's in charge around here," Ernie added. "I'll bet the chief is about ready to can him."

"He won't need to, if I get there first," Roy said.

Kara turned to Neil. "You're going after Sean too? Who will be next? My mother? Where will it end?"

At this challenge, Neil's mood seemed to change, a thunderous expression twisting his features. "Enough." He waved the gun at Kara. "Let's go. I want to show you the old waterwheel." His cruel laugh chilled her. "A private tour."

Under normal circumstances Kara would have been interested and charmed to see the process that had powered the mill in its heyday, but she certainly wasn't now. She had a sinking feeling that his plan involved more than showing her the antique wheel. If she ended up in that frigid river water, she would die within minutes.

And Neil would get away with another murder. This time premeditated.

Sean scanned the old mill as he drove the cruiser across the bridge. He didn't see any lights, except at the entrances. Was Kara even here? Maybe Michelle had heard wrong.

But then he remembered the new construction in the other wing, which was reached by going around back. Could they be there? The chief had mentioned that the former production space was being converted into apartments. But Sean had gotten the impression that they were far from complete. Surely it was rather premature for a tour.

Slowing to a crawl, Sean eased the cruiser into the parking lot, straining to try to pick out Kara's vehicle. It wasn't there, and the parking lot was empty, so he continued around the building.

His heart jumped when he saw her car next to an entrance. A light burned over the door, but otherwise, the building was dark. A couple of trucks were parked at the edge of the lot near some dumpsters, so he went to check them out.

One he recognized, and satisfaction burned. It was the black pickup that he'd been searching for, the one he'd chased out by Dead Man's Curve. He'd known he'd find it sooner or later, and its presence now was an indication that it was the vehicle that had menaced Kara and her mother.

Sean parked the cruiser near the door, but before he got out, he radioed in to tell dispatch where he was. He told them he was checking out the property, and he didn't need backup at the moment. After all, he might go in and find Kara having a perfectly fine time.

But his deepest instincts told him otherwise.

The door was open, so he walked in, taking care not to make much noise. He listened closely but heard nothing. The entrance hall was empty, and he had a choice of three doors leading deeper into the building. Remembering the dark windows in front, he went straight ahead. Neil and Kara must be at the back of the building, which bordered the river. Before Benedict Fuller started renovating the place, a teenage Sean and his friends had explored the property. They hadn't vandalized anything. They'd just been curious about the mysterious behemoth in the middle of town.

The corridor ahead of him was long, the only light filtering in through double doors at the end, and he found himself holding his breath. Where was she? The doors on both sides were firmly closed, and when he peeked into one, he found an empty space. These had to be future apartments.

He slowed even more the closer he got to the end, almost tiptoeing, then began to edge along the wall. He didn't want them to see movement through the windows. Not until he assessed the situation.

Craning his neck, he peered inside. He saw the backs of two men, standing a short distance from the doors. Their attention was on the other side of the room. Sean lifted his chin another inch or two to see. The scene before him drove ice into his veins.

Kara, standing near a large table. And Neil, training a handgun on her. Neil waved it, indicating Kara should move.

Where was he planning to take her?

Sean definitely needed that backup now, but rather than use his walkie-talkie and alert the people in the room, he sent a text on the secure message server to the state police.

Then he formulated a plan.

Kara's mind raced. How was she going to get out of this? She knew she couldn't leave the room with Neil, and she wasn't going down without a fight. Kara wondered if her aunt had fought back. A groan rose in her throat. She couldn't think about that right now.

"Come on," Neil growled at her.

Time was running out. She thought about the contents of her handbag. Nothing much except a pen. And a bottle of perfume—

The room's double doors burst open, and Sean marched inside.

With grunts of surprise, the two watchdogs turned to face him, fists clenched.

Sean hit Roy in the jaw. The man went down like a log, his head hitting the floor with an audible *thump*.

Kara didn't wait to see what happened to Ernie. She retrieved her perfume and sprayed Neil right in the eyes with it, then picked up a heavy tape measure from the table and hurled it at him.

The tape measure struck Neil square on the side of the head. Shouting with pain, he staggered sideways and dropped the gun, which skittered across the floor.

Kara made a mad scramble and grabbed the gun, holding it steady with both hands. "Put your hands up." Every ounce of her anger over the deaths of her father and aunt was in her tone.

Neil glared at her and made a feint toward her.

Kara cocked the gun. "Just try me. My daddy taught me how to shoot, and I always hit the bull's-eye."

Neil put his hands up, still glaring, but he didn't make another move.

Kara didn't even glance away while Sean read the men their rights—so he had managed to subdue Ernie too. She heard Sean cuff Roy and Ernie with zip ties.

Sean strode over to the table, his own gun drawn. "Are you all right?"

"I think so," Kara said, a tremble working its way into her voice. "Neil was going to kill me. He was going to make me jump into the river. And he caused my dad to crash his car."

"I guessed something like that happened," Sean said. "I read your father's file tonight. I'll take it from here. Good job." He removed the metal cuffs from his belt and snapped them with a satisfying click onto Neil's wrists. "Neil Fuller, you are under arrest."

Sean was relieved that the promised backup arrived swiftly. It was the state police, who had jurisdiction over serious felonies and capital crimes.

The troopers were taking Kara's statement and preparing to transfer the three criminals to the county jail when Chief Colton walked in.

"What's going on?" the chief demanded of Sean. "Why didn't you call me first?"

"The state had jurisdiction." Resting his hands on his hips, Sean studied his uncle's face. "Neil Fuller almost killed Kara Foxworth tonight. If I hadn't gotten here when I did . . ." He swallowed. What might have been would haunt his nightmares for quite a while, he suspected.

The chief made a scoffing sound, running his hand over his thinning hair. He wasn't in uniform, his casual attire signaling that he'd come from home. "Why would Neil do a thing like that?"

"You tell me," Sean said. "He had a gun pointed right at her, indicating the threat of deadly force, right? Only I wasn't going to wait until he pulled the trigger to intervene." He thought of something else. "That was you talking to Neil the other night, wasn't it? While I was on patrol."

The chief didn't seem to have an answer. Instead, he evaded Sean's gaze and glanced around the room.

"I want a lawyer!" Neil bellowed. "My father will have your job for this."

Chief Colton flinched, seeming to fold in on himself.

"And you're entitled to an attorney, as you were told," a trooper replied, his voice bland and obviously unimpressed. "You can make a phone call after you're booked. Come along now."

Neil was escorted out between two troopers, glaring daggers at Sean and Kara as he went.

Kara, who had finished giving her statement, slid off a stool at the table and came over. "What happened tonight was the tip of the iceberg. But I'll bet you know all about it, don't you, Chief?"

Sean had listened to the statements given by Ernie and Roy. Ernie had admitted to leaving Kara the threats and attacking her in the sugar shack after Roy had sent her there and alerted him. Roy had been responsible for the break-ins at Angela's, including the assault on Sean. Roy also owned the old black pickup, and it had been used to push Angela's car over the edge.

"Those evil men murdered my aunt and pushed her and her car into that ravine," Kara continued. "Why? Because she figured out Benedict and Everett's little scheme. Two upright citizens." She shook her head. "Who would have guessed?"

"What are you talking about?" the chief asked.

"Neil told me everything," Kara replied. "You know, while he was planning to kill me too. Something about skimming money from the college endowment funds and funneling it into his father's companies. And I'm sure once they do some digging, how and when won't be too hard to figure out."

The chief didn't respond.

Her smile was wry. "I told the state troopers all about it. One of them said something about a forensics team going in after a warrant is signed. And from what I overheard, your buddy Neil decided to cooperate. His temper tantrum a bit ago was all for show. He's going to flip on you to try to get his own sentence reduced."

Chief Colton visibly deflated under the barrage of Kara's revelations. "I had no idea," he said weakly.

Sean knew his uncle was lying. "That's not true, and you know it," Sean said, putting a hand on his shoulder. "They couldn't have gone as far as they did without your help. Or at least you turning a blind eye." His voice was gentle. Despite being appalled and outraged by his uncle's betrayal, he didn't believe in kicking a man when he was down. And his uncle was definitely going down. The chief's thirty-year legacy was sadly tainted now, and he would probably go to jail.

Sean bit his lip, scarcely believing what he had to say next to his own uncle. His heart practically tore in his chest with grief and sorrow. But what could he do? His uncle had made his own choices. "If I were you, I would cooperate fully. Maybe they'll take it into consideration."

The chief nodded. "I know this isn't easy for you. But you're right. I'll go confess." His shoulders sagged in defeat. "Take care of your aunt for me, will you?" Then he paused. "The sad thing is, I could have retired. They paid me enough. But they wouldn't let me go yet. They were afraid a new chief might not be so cooperative. Maybe now Peggy can get her Florida sunshine. Without me."

Sean watched his uncle shamble away. He would fulfill the chief's request to take care of Aunt Peggy. Her heart would be broken by her husband's actions.

Kara leaned against Sean, wrapping an arm around his waist. "That must have been really hard. I'm so sorry for you. It's a tragedy all around."

He gazed into her sweet face. Here she was, comforting him, when she'd had so many devastating losses and revelations. Once again, his battered, bruised heart ached, but this time it was with love for this brave, beautiful, loyal woman. He didn't deserve her, but perhaps she'd have him anyway. He hoped so with every fiber of his being.

"You're one special person. Do you know that?" His voice was husky, and he had to clear his throat. "There's something I should have explained to you a long time ago."

"What is it?"

"Back in high school, I didn't start dating Tiffany until after we broke up," Sean said. "I would have never done something like that to you. I've wanted to tell you for years, but I was afraid you wouldn't believe me."

"At the time, I probably wouldn't have," she admitted. "I'm just glad it was only a rumor."

"When I saw Neil—" He halted for a moment, unable to talk. "I almost died."

She hugged him with both arms now.

In return, Sean embraced her, pulling her close.

"I prayed you'd come," Kara murmured. "Through this whole ordeal, you've been there for me every step of the way." Tears glittered in her eyes. "Please don't leave me again."

He tightened his arms around her. "I won't leave you. I'm yours forever. I promise."

Christmas carols played on the stereo, and a fire crackled in the woodstove, the perfect background for wrapping gifts. Kara couldn't believe that the holiday was tomorrow.

Tonight, she'd be attending a Christmas Eve service with Sean, her mother, and Nelson. They were eating together first, and savory aromas already drifted from the kitchen, where Nelson was helping her mom with the final touches on dinner. He'd been thrilled to be included in their Christmas Eve celebration.

It had been a few days since the showdown at the mill, but the scandal rocking Castlebridge was far from over. As Kara had told the chief, Neil's actions that night were merely the tip of the iceberg. Sean had some new developments that he'd promised to share tonight. The state police and other agencies had worked feverishly to put the case together.

Meanwhile, Kara and her mother had enjoyed Castlebridge Christmas Days. They'd done some more shopping, listened to carolers in the park, and attended a Nativity play at the church. She'd just applied tape to Sean's present when the doorbell rang. There he was now. She quickly set the colorful package under the tree and hurried to let him in.

"Merry Christmas," Sean said. Dressed for church, he was handsome in a suit, tie, and dress coat—but the Santa hat on his head provided a comical touch. He held several packages in his arms.

"Look at you," Kara said with a laugh. She stood on tiptoes and gave him a quick kiss. "Get inside before you freeze."

Sean grinned. "Guess what? It's starting to snow. Again." He entered the house, pausing to brush his feet on the rug. Then he slipped out of low rubber boots, leaving them on the rug to the side.

Kara poked her head out the front door and saw he was right. A dusting of fresh snow was already covering the sidewalks and roads, which had been clear an hour ago. She groaned. "Seriously? We already have two feet." She reached for the packages. "Let me have those so you can take off your coat."

He handed her the gifts and took off his coat, which he hung up on a peg. He rubbed his hands together. "Something smells great."

"Mom's making Cornish game hens," Kara said. "They're our Christmas Eve tradition." She moved toward the living room. "Come sit down. Want some hot apple cider?"

"Sounds good." Sean sat on the sofa, stretching his legs toward the warmth of the fire. "Ah, this is so nice."

Kara grabbed her empty mug and went into the kitchen. "Sean's here," she announced, going over to the slow cooker that held the cider. She ladled some into her mug and another waiting there for Sean.

"So I heard," her mother said, eyes twinkling. She opened the oven door and removed a roasting pan holding four tiny chickens. "These need to rest while I make gravy."

Nelson stood by the counter, a mixer in his hand, and smiled. "And I'm about to whip up my famous mashed potatoes."

"I love mashed potatoes. Is there anything else I can do?" Kara had already set the table in the dining alcove off the living room, using their best linens and dishes. That was also part of the tradition. Christmas Day was more relaxed, featuring lounging around, reading, and eating leftovers.

Her mother made a shooing motion. "No. Scoot. We have everything under control."

Kara carried the mugs back to the living room and handed one to Sean.

"Thanks." He patted the cushion beside him. "Join me?"

She sat down next to him. "How was your day?" He'd worked the day shift at the station.

After taking a sip of cider, Sean leaned his head back with a sigh. "Busy. Hard." After a pause, he said, "The select board named me acting chief."

"Congrats, I think." Yes, this was a promotion, but the circumstances of its award were certainly far from ideal.

He patted her knee, his smile wan. "Thanks. It's not anything I ever thought I wanted, even before this all went down. I was planning to apply to the state police academy and work on becoming a detective. But now I think Castlebridge might be where I belong."

"You'd be a great detective," Kara pointed out. "I think you've proven that already."

"Well, I had major help," he said. "Maybe you should apply too." His smile was teasing.

"No thanks," Kara said with a mock shudder. "I prefer investigating library patron inquiries." She touched his arm. "Speaking of which, there's an opening at the local library. I already sent in my résumé."

A smile broke across his face. "So you're staying?"

"If I get the job." Kara couldn't hold back her excitement. "It sounds promising. They already called me for an interview. I'm going after New Year's." She'd had to take another day of leave from her present job, but she had accrued plenty of time off. And she wouldn't be leaving her school in the lurch. The substitute librarian who filled in for her had been hoping for a full-time position to open up, and Kara was sure she'd get the job.

Kara and her mother had talked about it and agreed that Angela's house would be a perfect place for Kara to move into if the job came through. She loved this neighborhood, which was now safe from development by the Fullers.

"That's wonderful," Sean said. "Now if I could figure out my own life."

"You will," Kara said warmly. She had every faith in Sean's decision-making abilities. "So your uncle is officially done with the department?" That had been a foregone conclusion after the chief's arrest. He'd never serve in law enforcement again.

"Yeah," Sean said, his voice sad. "They let him resign, although they certainly had grounds to fire him."

"What about the others?" she asked.

"They got them last night. Everett was on his way to Canada. But Benedict and Walter were here in town. I guess they knew better than to run. I was surprised about Walter. He always handled our legal business. By the way, Tiffany came forward. She's going to testify."

"That's great," Kara said. "Neil told me that Angela had found key evidence in Walter's files. That's how she put it all together."

Sean turned his head and studied her, his expression somber. "In the course of all this, the state police and I took another look at everything. One thing we verified through phone records was that Angela *was* on her way to a meeting with the Vermont State Attorney General's office."

Kara sucked in a breath. "She was going to blow the whistle, like we thought."

"When we pressed Walter about the sequence of events, he admitted that she'd been acting odd for a while, but he got really suspicious when she scheduled an unexpected day off in the middle of the week. In ten years of working for him, she'd never done that. So he gave her something to do in another part of the office and snooped around her desk. He found her phone and went through her call logs. He knew the state attorney's office number, of course."

Kara was staggered to hear this about the attorney she had respected. To think that Walter had extended his condolences to her and her mother without even a hint of his duplicity. Aunt Angela must have been crushed when she'd realized her boss was a criminal.

"There's only one missing piece of evidence," Sean said. "Not that it's essential now. The state team is digging into the college financials, and I have no doubt they'll find what they need. But everyone is wondering where the information Angela gathered went. Where she hid it."

Her gaze fell on the covered bridge picture, propped on top of a bookcase, ready for Nelson to take home later. "I wonder." Kara set her mug down and got to her feet.

"Where are you going?" Sean asked, curiosity in his voice.

"You'll see," she said, not wanting to say anything in case she was wrong. She lifted the picture off the bookcase, once more admiring the skill and artistry her aunt had used in creating the piece. It was beautiful.

Kara carried the picture back to the couch, where she set it upside down on the coffee table. Brown paper covered the back of the embroidery, sealing it into the glass and frame. She hated to rip off the paper, so she got up and went to the hall table, where she found a metal letter opener. She drew the sharp point along the paper, tracing the edge of the frame.

"You think something is in there?" Sean asked.

Kara nodded, excitement building as she realized the backing was far thicker than normal. Her aunt had put something between the paper and the back of the artwork. "Go get Mom and Nelson," she said. "They need to see this."

After Sean returned with the others, she carefully cut all the way around and then lifted the thick brown paper out of the way. A sheaf of papers was behind it, fitting perfectly against the embroidered cloth.

Her mother gasped, then grabbed Nelson's arm. "Angela's evidence."

Nelson blinked, his eyes damp. "She must have sensed something might happen to her. She was counting on us to make sure the truth came out."

"Hold on," Sean said. "Don't touch the papers yet. I'll get a pair of gloves and an evidence bag from my truck." He hurried out of the room.

A few moments later, Sean returned. He used his phone to take a couple of photographs, and then he put gloves on. Carefully, so carefully, he lifted out the sheaf of papers.

One glance was all it took. Angela had written a document detailing everything she knew—from the first time Walter received a covert payment from Benedict Fuller. She had photocopies of a second set of books Walter had hidden at the office. These detailed the true picture regarding the endowment funds.

"I'm sure this will all tally with what the forensics team digs up," Sean said. "I'll call the state police detective in the morning."

Tears of relief filled Kara's eyes. "We did it, Aunt Angela," she whispered. "It's finally over."

After a delicious dinner, Kara rode with Sean to the police station and then to church. The snow was still falling, and downtown was more magical than ever. But maybe that was because it was Christmas Eve, one of the most wonderful days of the year.

The church they attended was near the town green, a classic white clapboard building with antique stained glass windows and a tall steeple. They parked and joined the throngs of churchgoers streaming along the sidewalks and up the wide granite steps, many stopping to say hello and wish one another a merry Christmas.

Her mother had saved them spots in their favorite pew, and they slid in beside her and Nelson. The church was tastefully decorated with garlands of pine, groups of small Christmas trees, and clusters of candles. In the front of the sanctuary near the altar, a crèche stood in pride of place.

People continued to filter in, and soon the pews were full. The organist in the loft had been playing a soft prelude, and as the minister prepared to enter, she shifted to one of Kara's favorite carols.

As voices rose in song, capably led by the choir, Kara's heart lifted in sheer bliss along with the music. *O come, all ye faithful, joyful and triumphant!*

With her beloved mother on her left and Sean, the love of her life, on her right, Kara was home for Christmas in Castlebridge, right where she belonged.

Up to this point, we've been doing all the writing. Now it's *your* turn!

Tell us what you think about this book, the characters, the bad guy, or anything else you'd like to share with us about this series. We can't wait to hear from *you!*

Log on to give us your feedback at:

https://www.surveymonkey.com/r/sweetintrigue

Annie's FICTION